DANGER EVERYWHERE

Wild Bill's room was basic but clean: an iron bedstead with a feather mattress, a ladderback chair, a washstand with a metal bowl and pitcher, a few nails driven into the wall for hanging up clothes and gunbelts. The lock was flimsy, so he tilted the chair under the doorknob to reinforce it.

The window, too, bothered him—there was a clear angle of fire toward the bed. So Bill decided to drag the bed to the other wall.

That was how he discovered the ingenious death trap.

Bill spotted it the moment he pulled the bedstead away from the wall. A can of blasting powder had been placed under the bed. A short fuse was paid out from the can to a knothole in the room's front wall. It could easily and quickly be lighted from outside. . . .

Other *Leisure* books by Judd Cole:

The *Wild Bill* Series:
 #1: DEAD MAN'S HAND
 #2: THE KINKAID COUNTY WAR
 #3: BLEEDING KANSAS
 #4: YUMA BUSTOUT
 #5: SANTA FE DEATH TRAP
 #6: BLACK HILLS HELLHOLE
 #7: POINT RIDER

The *Cheyenne* series:
 #1: ARROW KEEPER
 #2: DEATH CHANT
 #3: RENEGADE JUSTICE
 #4: VISION QUEST
 #5: BLOOD ON THE PLAINS
 #6: COMANCHE RAID
 #7: COMANCHEROS
 #8: WAR PARTY
 #9: PATHFINDER
 #10: BUFFALO HIDERS
 #11: SPIRIT PATH
 #12: MANKILLER
 #13: WENDIGO MOUNTAIN
 #14: DEATH CAMP
 #15: RENEGADE NATION
 #16: ORPHAN TRAIN
 #17: VENGEANCE QUEST
 #18: WARRIOR FURY
 #19: BLOODY BONES CANYON
 #20: RENEGADE SIEGE
 #21: RIVER OF DEATH
 #22: DESERT MANHUNT

WILD BILL
GUN LAW

JUDD COLE

LEISURE BOOKS NEW YORK CITY

A LEISURE BOOK®

May 2001

Published by

Dorchester Publishing Co., Inc.
276 Fifth Avenue
New York, NY 10001

ISBN 0-8439-4874-4

The name "Leisure Books" and the stylized "L" with design are trademarks of Dorchester Publishing Co., Inc.

Printed in the United States of America.

Visit us on the web at www.dorchesterpub.com.

GUN LAW

Chapter One

"Damn you straight to hell, you little ink-slinger," J. B. Hickok fumed as he and young Joshua Robinson emerged from the Bluebird Café and started across Denver's busy Division Street. "I am *not—*"

Wild Bill snatched the newspaper out from under Josh's arm and read out loud, " 'reluctant to fight a man if it means Wild Bill will get his clothes mussed up.' "

Hickok flung the paper back at the journalist. "Katy Christ! You make me sound like some fussing female."

Even as he raised this objection, however, Hickok frowned at all the mud caking his new oxblood boots.

"This street's a reg'lar pigsty," he complained. "They need to ditch it so the water runs off."

Hickok's gunmetal-blue eyes stayed in constant scanning motion. The 1870s had ushered in a boom, and Denver had grown far beyond its original boundaries as a rough-and-tumble mining camp. Horses, freight wagons, drummers' vans, buggies, and pedestrians all churned up the mud, and so many people forced Wild Bill to an unrelenting vigilance. Fame, he had discovered, was not just a fickle whore but a dangerous one.

Among the many characters in this press of humanity, a stocky man wearing a buffalo coat caught Joshua's attention. He was thickset and tall and thumped along the boardwalk with a noticeable limp. A thick shock of silver hair hung like a curtain fringe below his flap hat.

Hickok had noticed him too. His eyes narrowed slightly.

"That coat," he remarked casually to Josh, "seems a mite warm for September."

Josh caught Bill's drift. Denver, like more and more big cities in the West, had recently passed an ordinance against carrying guns in public. That's why Hickok had on his long canvas duster—to conceal the ivory-grip Colt .44s that he refused to surrender.

By now the two friends had also reached the boardwalk. Just as they did, the man in the buffalo coat angled into the foyer of the Cattleman's Palace Hotel, apparently unaware of the two men. They entered behind him and watched him limp toward the front desk, where two clerks in sleeve garters and silk vests waited behind the guest register.

"He's carrying no poke, either," Bill remarked, more curious than wary. "That limp . . . He seems familiar somehow."

But the stranger paid them no heed as he fished a silver dollar out of his pocket and signed the register. Bill seemed to lose interest in him.

"C'mon, Longfellow," he told Josh, steering him toward the slatted batwings of the hotel saloon. "I *ought* to belt your head off for all that claptrap you write about me. Instead I'll stand you to a whiskey, because you really are a talented scribbler when you ain't telling lies about me."

"I just hold a mirror up to nature, Bill."

"Yeah? Hold your lips up to my ass."

Both men laughed. They had a quick drink at the bar, where two customers recognized Hickok and immediately asked him if they could touch him for luck. He good-naturedly shook their hands—Wild Bill Hickok had escaped certain death so often, he had become the nation's walking rabbit's foot. The hotel barber had even begun to save Bill's clipped hair, tying the locks up with string and selling them as talismans.

Bill took the newspaper from Josh again and read: " 'Neither the Colt .44 nor the Winchester rifle is among the three inventions that are winning the Wild West. It is barbed wire, the portable windmill, and the steel plow that are taming this rugged territory.' "

Hickok looked at the kid and nodded.

" 'S'true, Joshua. Time is closing in on the old fossils like me."

"Maybe so," Josh said. "But stories about plows don't sell newspapers."

"Well," Bill announced reluctantly after two fortifying shots of Old Taylor bourbon, "time to see if Pinkerton left a note under my door. The old skinflint has another job for me. Something about a rustlers' camp in Wyoming."

The Palace featured one of the new hydraulic elevators, and Wild Bill and Joshua rode it up to the fifth floor, where they each had a room.

The car jerk-bumped to a stop, and the kid operating it pulled the door open for them. The two friends stepped out, and before he could even blink, Wild Bill felt a cold gun muzzle pressing into the side of his neck!

About four hundred miles northeast of Denver, in the Black Hills of Dakota, the light of late afternoon was taking on a mellow richness just before sunset.

A sturdy Concord express coach pulled by six horses eased into a dogleg bend in the road, tug chains rattling, driver lashing the lead team with a blacksnake whip.

"Gee up!" he shouted at the fresh team. "He-yah! He-yah!"

A guard with a 12-gauge double-barrel shotgun across his thighs sat on the box beside the driver. Another guard, armed with a Sharps Big Fifty, sat on the top seat behind them, facing the other way. This coach carried no ticketed passengers—only a reinforced strongbox containing bars of newly smelted gold.

Canyon walls marked with striation sur-rounded this bend in the trail. It was good ambush country, and all three men were taut with vigilance.

Swaying on its leather braces, the coach careened out of the long turn.

"God A'mighty!" the gray-bearded driver exclaimed, suddenly throwing his weight onto the brake handle. "Haw!" he roared at the team, tugging hard on the reins.

The body of a man, obviously shot in the back, lay sprawled front-down across the trail. The back of his shirt was caked with dried blood. And alongside the trail lay his likewise dead horse. Flies swarmed all over it.

"He never even seen it coming," the guard with the shotgun said grimly as the coach pulled up just short of the human corpse. "Lookit—whoever drilled him even took his boots. Poor bastard."

"I'll take a look," the driver said, wrapping the reins around the brake handle. "I pray God I don't know him."

Just in case the highwaymen were still lurking nearby, both guards remained atop the coach, scanning the dusty bushes and scrub oaks that crowded the trail on both sides.

The driver knelt, placed a hand on one of the dead man's shoulders, and started to turn him over. In less time than a heartbeat the "dead man" came up to a sitting position, a Smith & Wesson Volcanic spitting muzzle fire.

A neat hole appeared in the driver's forehead,

11

a thin worm of blood spurting out of it even as he toppled in a heap, heels scratching the dirt before he died.

Before either guard could get his rifle on bead, more hammering gunfire erupted from the bushes. One guard, heart ripped open, plummeted dead to the ground under the left front wheel. The second cried out in pain and dropped his weapon when a bullet punched into his left forearm.

The team, panicked by the gunfire, tried to spurt forward. But the shooter in the road plugged one of the wheel horses, and the dragging weight in the traces, plus the drag of the brake, held the coach after it skidded only a few feet.

A huge, barrel-chested man wearing range clothes stepped out from the screening timber, his six-shooter still emitting curls of blue smoke. The smell of spent powder sweetened the air.

"All right, mister!" shouted Sandy Urbanski, the one wearing the blood-caked shirt. "Do everything I tell you, and do it in a puffin' hurry, or I'll irrigate your guts."

The guard had slapped his right hand over the wound to his arm. Blood fountained past his fingers.

"You will anyhow," he retorted. "Neither one of you bastards has bothered to pull his neckerchief up."

Urbanski's gun jumped in his fist, and the guard's wide-brimmed hat flew off his head.

"Cork it, hero," he snarled, malice gleaming

in his eyes. "Just do what you're told. Ricky," he added, looking at his partner, "go fetch the buckboard while our big brave hero takes that gold out of the strongbox for us."

"I ain't got no key for the strongbox," the wounded man pointed out, speaking past pain-gritted teeth.

"Well, I have," Urbanski told him. "Move it!"

The guard, favoring his wounded arm, climbed down. Urbanski flipped him the key, which he caught with one bloody hand. As the guard stacked the gold bars out in the road, Ur-banski's hard-bitten eyes of a cold killer watched everything from a weathered, cruelly handsome face. The deep, furled knife scar un-der his left eye was the legacy of a fight with an Apache down in Sonora.

"You goddamn fools," he taunted the guard. "Any simple son of a bitch can put on a bloody shirt. And that sorrel horse the flies're eating is one of your own, stole from a way station. Too bad you boys are so hawg-stupid, ain't it?"

The guard's eyes cut to the bodies in the road. "Whoever you are, you'll stretch hemp for this."

Urbanski's smile was a scornful twist. "You think? Well now, I'm wettin' my drawers in fear. Damn shame, though, you won't be around to watch me dance on air, hey?"

Crushed shrubbery crackled as Rick Collins drove the hidden buckboard out beside the coach. The big man had blunt features deeply pockmarked from a near-fatal bout with small-pox.

13

"Load 'em up," Urbanski ordered their prisoner.

The heavy bars were a struggle with only one good arm, but the guard finally managed to get them loaded. Collins tossed an old horse blanket over them.

"Mister," the guard said to Urbanski, sleeving sweat off his face. "I know you're going to kill me. Can I have just a minute to get straight with my maker?"

Urbanski put a pious look on his face. "Well, bless my soul! Our hero's a holy man, too. You want me and Rick to sing a hymn, too?"

The guard stoically said nothing.

"Go to it, holy man," Urbanski urged him. "We'll wait until you're done praying. Least we can do for a Christian."

However, the very moment the guard lowered his head to pray, Urbanski shot him between the eyes.

"Now, ain't that a pure-dee shame?" he asked his partner. "The poor bastard died with all his sins still fresh on him. Well, it don't matter, because Hell ain't *half* full."

Chapter Two

"Jumpin' Jehosaphat!" Joshua exclaimed, recognizing the man who had just ambushed Wild Bill in the hallway. It was the man in the shaggy buffalo coat.

"Hickok, you shouldn't ought to be so careless," the man warned in a voice made husky by years of strong tobacco.

"Friend," Bill replied with remarkable calmness, "if you meant to kill me, it would be over by now. So what's your grift?"

The man holstered his weapon, and a wide grin split his weather-rawed face. "Look close, you woman-haired, perfumed dandy. Has fame made you forget *all* of us no-count working stiffs?"

Josh watched his hero study the man's face a moment.

"Well, God kiss me!" Hickok suddenly exclaimed, seizing the man's leathery paw and shaking it. "Joshua Robinson, meet Mr. Leland Langford. When I was just a mere chit of a boy like you, he and I drove stagecoaches and freight wagons along the Old Mormon Trail to Utah."

"Sainted backsides, but we *had* some wild times, didn't we, Billy? We didn't just raise hell—by God, we also *tilted* it a few feet."

"You've got fat, you bucket of guts," Bill told him bluntly.

"Huh. I'm still strong as horse radish," Leland boasted. "Don't *even* make me kick your skinny ass."

"Let's head to my room," Bill suggested. "I've got a bottle of coffin varnish and three jolt glasses."

The three men headed down the long hallway. Candles flickered in sconces along the walls, their flames reflected in the polish of the floor and glowing like rubescent embers.

"You still a teamster?" Wild Bill asked his friend.

"And then some, b'hoy. I'm part owner of the Overland Line."

Hickok loosed a whistle, and Joshua knew why: Overland was a major stage-and-freight line west of the Mississippi River.

The three men stopped outside Wild Bill's door while he fished the key from his pocket. From long habit Bill did not simply unlock the door and go in. First he studied the very top of the door, where he had fastened a short piece of string between the door frame and the door with two pinches of soft sealing wax. It was still intact.

Nonetheless, once inside the room the first thing Wild Bill did was step out onto the scrolled-iron balcony to check for intruders.

"All clear," he announced. "Gents, let's imbibe a spot of the giant killer."

"Toss me the makings, Bill," Leland said.

"I got tired of building cigarettes," Bill explained. "All I can give you is a Mexican skinny."

He slid a cheroot out of his vest pocket and offered it. But Leland scowled. "Christ, you *have* turned female on me. Never mind, I've got my pipe."

Bill poured shots of bourbon all around, and the three men clinked glasses as he proposed a toast: "To dark bars and fair women."

Josh was not a veteran drinker, and the strong liquor burned a straight line to his gut. He coughed, his eyes filming, and the other two laughed good-naturedly.

"The Philadelphia Kid here," Bill explained to his old trail companion, "is fresh off ma's milk. A newspaper writer who's been to high school and parley-voos French."

"It's men like him who create the soul of a nation, J. B. Not to mention they make you famous."

"There's that," Wild Bill conceded. "But I still like this one. He's a fair shot, and he's got more guts than a smokehouse. Saved my life up in Miles City."

17

But Bill's gunmetal eyes were fixed speculatively on Leland. "Let's get down to cases, old son. What's your trouble? You didn't look me up just to shoot at rovers."

Leland had already shrugged out of his heavy coat and tossed it onto the bed. Now he slacked into a chair near the door, scrubbing his face with his hands. Josh noticed that his eyes were suddenly grave.

"J. B., do you stay abreast of financial matters?"

Hickok snorted. "I know when my pockets are empty. Why do you ask?"

"Right now the U.S. Treasury is facing a real monetary crisis. You've noticed, of course, how eastern money is replacing gold coins."

Hickok nodded. By "eastern money," Leland meant paper banknotes that were backed by gold reserves, which were presently being printed in Denver.

"Most folks don't cotton to folding money," Leland went on. "But the government is trying to protect the country against gold-hoarding. With paper they can keep the Rockefellers and Vanderbilts from what amounts to taking over the country."

By now Joshua was focused like a hound on point. He sensed a big story here—a story as big as America itself.

"Makes sense so far," Bill said. "But you're still too far north for me. How do I mix in it?"

"The Dakota Division of the Overland Line has been critical to the government. It's been our job to get smelted gold from the Black Hills to the mint here in Denver."

Wild Bill frowned. "But the Kansas Pacific has a spur line that pushes northeast to Rapid City. Why wouldn't they use the rails?"

"At first they did. But after two holdups, with the tracks ripped up both times and causing derailments, the railroad barons rebelled. Twelve people were killed the last time, and it scared away passengers. Congress has no authority to order railroad cooperation except in time of war."

Bill nodded. "Let me guess. Now Overland has had a robbery?"

"Several," Joshua chimed in. "It's been all over the newspapers."

"What's not in the newspapers, though, is word of a new government regulation," Leland said. "From now on, the mint can't print any paper money until the gold backing it is actually locked up in their vault. All these heists have drastically slowed down paper issue; matter fact, it's almost been brought to a screeching whoa. If the paper-money plan fails, this great republic could someday be taken over by a gold-rich tyrant. It's happened before in Europe."

Joshua felt his nape tingle at the importance of what Leland had just said. America was still, politically speaking, an experiment in democratic freedom—an experiment that could still easily fail. The spirit of '76 could end up in the ash bin of history, defeated by the same monarchic despotism the Founding Fathers defeated.

"Leland," Bill interjected, "I'm as patriotic as the next jasper. Don't forget I wore Union blue during the Great Rebellion, even though I'm a strong states' rights man. But what's *my* mix in all this? Get down out of the clouds."

Leland frowned, a deep crease appearing between his eyebrows. Josh watched worry suddenly mold his face.

"Bill, I know damn good and well who's in charge of the holdups. But I can't *prove* it, damn my eyes. It's a slick weasel named Gil Brennan. He was once the Dakota Division agent for Overland. A while back we were having a lot of problems with that sector—mailbags missing, filthy way-stations, passengers getting robbed and beaten, drivers getting drunk on the job. You know what they say—a new broom sweeps clean. I fired Brennan and most of the men he hired."

Bill bit down on a cheroot, then thumb-scratched a lucifer to light it. "So now it's an inside job, or as good as. This Brennan—he and his gunsels know the stageline business inside out, making it hard to protect the shipments or nab him in the act."

Leland nodded. "Brennan is slick as snot on a doorknob. Nothing has worked. He's got sharpshooters from somewhere—men who slaughtered a military escort without ever once showing themselves. So we dropped the escort plan and switched to secret gold shipments in stagecoaches instead of freight wagons."

"And that didn't work," Bill supplied, "because Brennan is getting word from inside, right?"

Leland nodded again. "And what makes it double rough is that he's got his toadies in the Army, too, so we can't be certain it's Overland employees tipping him off."

Bill mulled all this while his forgotten cigar went out.

"All right," he said finally. "Obviously you want me to do something about it. What's your plan?"

"You were once a first-rate driver. More important, you're the best shootist in America. We want you to hire on and push a bullion coach through the Dakota sector. One loaded with more gold than we've ever hauled at one time. One Brennan and his gun-throwers won't be able to resist heisting."

Wild Bill frowned. "You call that a plan? Sounds to me like I'm just the meat that feeds the tiger."

Leland shook his head. "You won't be a one-man outfit. I'm working with General Stanley Durant on this. He's the C.O. of Fort Bridger. There'll be two men from his command, dressed in mufti and traveling as passengers on the coach. These are top-shelf marksmen and battle-hardened veterans. So good with fire-arms that they shoot in national tournaments for the Army."

Bill looked skeptical. "All well and good. Let's say we push this coach through. How does that solve your problem in the long haul?"

Leland nodded in Joshua's direction. "Power

of the press, J. B. The point isn't just to get this one coach through. We want you to bust up Gil Brennan's ring and kill as many of them as you can. That'll send an unequivocal message to any other would-be gangs: Steal gold from the U.S. Treasury, and you'll face the harshest and most final law in the West: gun law."

Bill chewed up the end of his unlit cigar while he rolled the decision in his mind.

"You do know," he said to Leland, "that I'm working for Allan Pinkerton right now?"

"Sure I know. He's already been contacted. We'll pay his usual agency fee. And *you* will be on double wages. We match his pay dollar for dollar."

Hickok's face suddenly came alive with interest. "You'll pay me eight dollars a day?"

Leland nodded and played his trump card: "Plus a two-hundred-dollar bonus if that gold reaches Denver. As well as stock options in the company that could make you rich in old age."

"I ain't going to make 'old age,'" Bill said matter-of-factly. "I'll never reach age forty. I'll be plugged in the back long before that. But never mind all that—the pay is damn good, and that bonus will stake me at the card table. Just one more question: Who's riding the hot seat?"

Bill meant the shotgun rider. Leland shook his head. "You know the custom, J. B. Each driver picks his own."

Wild Bill nodded, satisfied. "I've got a man in mind, if he's still alive."

He looked at Josh. "How 'bout you, Longfellow? Deal you in?"

"You kidding? Try and stop me. It's an exclusive for the *New York Herald*."

Hickok grinned, strong white teeth flashing under his mustache. "Told you he's got a set on him," he told Leland. "Think you can maybe wangle a little pay for him, too?"

"Consider it done. We need a good reporter anyway, and you say this one can shoot. Four dollars a day sound good, lad?"

Josh goggled at the sum. "Yes, *sir*. The *Herald* only pays me eighty dollars a month."

"Good. I'll be in touch with both of you before I head back to Dakota. I'll have advance wages and railroad tickets for you. You'll see me again when you get out there."

Handshakes all around sealed the deal.

"Boys," Leland told them as he grabbed his coat off the bed, ready to leave, "it ain't my fortunes I'm worried about. You know, not very long ago more than six hundred thousand men died to hold this republic together. If the gold standard fails, and this nation with it, they died for nothing. And so did Abraham Lincoln. Godspeed to both of you."

Chapter Three

The five of them met secretly in rolling hill country sliced by gullies washed red with eroded soil: Gil Brennan, his chief henchmen Sandy Urbanski and Rick Collins, and two soldiers newly arrived in the Black Hills from Fort Bridger, Sergeant John Saville and Corporal Dan Appling. The soldiers had been detached for temporary duty and were under orders to wear civilian disguises.

"You've no doubt whatsoever," Brennan repeated, "that Leland hired Hickok?"

John Saville shook his head adamantly. He was pallid and stout, posing as a preacher; he wore clergy black with a starched white collar.

"Durant didn't tell us that, Mr. Brennan, no. But Danny here is the company clerk for our regiment. He heard General Durant's aide-de-camp mention it."

Gil Brennan nodded, his long aristocratic face more thoughtful than troubled. He wore a vermilion ranch suit and an expensive alpaca coat.

"It makes perfect sense," he conceded. "Hickok used to drive for the Midland Line's New Mexico Division. His passengers, I've been told, never lost a dollar in a holdup. Before that, he rode Pony Express and never lost a piece of mail."

"Don'tcha think, boss," Rick Collins suggested, "we best let this coach go?"

Collins was a stupid man, and usually Brennan had low tolerance for stupidity. But he had once witnessed it with his own eyes when Rick picked a blacksmith's anvil up two feet off the ground to win a strong-man contest in nearby Belle Fourche. He might not be the sharpest knife in the drawer, but such strength made him useful in a pinch. He was also an excellent shot with a rifle.

"Let not your hearts be troubled, gentlemen," he assured them. "J. B. Hickok is a formidable man, yes. And no doubt he'll select a likewise formidable shotgun rider. But they won't be expecting trouble from in their very midst."

He nodded at the two soldiers, both of whom would be posing as passengers on Hickok's coach. Saville's companion, Corporal Dan Appling, would be disguised as a toupee salesman. He was a rabbit-faced man wearing a straw boater and a cheap broadcloth suit. Even now he carried his straw sample case. But in reality, both men were among the U.S. Army's top pistol marksmen and competed annually in tournaments.

Urbanski snorted his contempt for all this. He was his usual sullen and apathetic self. He considered "meetings" strictly for women.

"Way I see it," he told his employer, "bribing these two target-poppers onto our side just means less swag for the rest of us. So I'm goin' up agin' Hickok for a smaller share. Why *not* let this stage get through to Denver? There'll be others."

Anger at Urbanski made Brennan's eyebrows arch, and his thin-lipped mouth set itself hard. He figured the man who paid the piper should also call the tunes. But he reminded himself this bunch weren't musicians, they were ice-cold killers, especially Urbanski. Discretion was the better part of valor.

"Sandy, are you forgetting the extra ten thousand dollars? The open bounty on Hickok?"

Urbanski's surly face came alive with sudden interest. "What bounty?"

"Hickok killed a rowdy cowboy while he was the starman in Abilene, Kansas. It was a fair fight, they say, but the cowboy's old man is a rich cattle baron in Texas. He'll pay ten thousand, no questions asked, to any man who brings him Hickok's head in a sack."

Urbanski's lips cleared his teeth in a wolf grin. "*Now* you're whistlin', boss. I mean to beat these soldier boys out for that money."

Brennan knew he could do it, too. Urbanski constantly practiced drawing and shooting. He had killed at least eight men in fair fights and shot twice that many in the back.

"That's fine by me," Brennan assured him. "So long as you remember the main goal is to get that gold. With Wild Bill Hickok in charge, they'll likely increase the gold shipment. The bigger the pie, the bigger the slices."

It was the size and number of those "slices" that forced Brennan's hand. This gold-heist ring involved not just himself and the actual holdup men, but an extensive ring of informers and accomplices, including some within the military. The only way to keep all these cutthroats from killing him was to go equal shares on each heist.

If things were different, he *would* just let that stage driven by Hickok get through safely. But the timing was against him. Gil Brennan needed at least another fifty thousand dollars, and quick, if he meant to go legitimate. He had an opportunity to buy up controlling interest in the Exposition Bank in San Francisco, his hometown. Once he did that, he would virtually own the city. But he had to move quick before foreign investors beat him to the bid.

"Hickok hasn't met you boys yet?" Brennan asked the soldiers.

"We were sent on ahead so nobody could connect us to him. By now he's met with Durant to work out their plan. He knows how we'll be disguised—that's how he'll know who we are."

Brennan mulled this for a minute. "Last time," he said, meaning the coach Sandy and

Judd Cole

Rick had just knocked off, "they tried an
express-messenger coach with no passengers.
Before that it was a military escort. Now they've
brought in a hired gun. I guess they figure if
they can't raise the bridge, they'll lower the
river. It means the government is getting desperate."

Urbanski snorted. "They can bring in Geron-
imo if they want. Won't be long, and Hickok will
be walking with his ancestors."

Brennan sent him a warning glance. "There's
a long list of dead men, Sandy, who've set out
to plant him. He was taken prisoner three times
during the War Between the States, but they
couldn't hold him. The man even survived a
grizzly bear attack in the Raton Pass. Don't sell
him short, or you *won't* live to regret it."

Brennan addressed all of them now. As he
spoke, one fist beat the palm of his other hand
to underscore his points.

"This thing won't be done slapdash. Personally, I'm hoping John and Danny here get a good
chance to sucker-shoot him. But if I rate Hickok
accurately, he won't completely trust anybody
but his shotgun rider. So before we even make
a play for that gold, we're going to throw him
off, get Hickok to lower his guard.

"How?" Urbanski demanded.

Brennan smiled. "That's easier than you
think. Don't forget he's walking into a stacked
deck, and *we're* holding all the aces."

"While you were on your way up here, Jimmy,"
Wild Bill explained, "Gil Brennan's gang struck

28

again. It happened just southwest of Rapid City. The driver and two guards murdered. The exact value of the gold wasn't mentioned in the story."

"And you're sure it was an inside job?" asked Jimmy Davis.

Hickok nodded, his vigilant eyes in motion as the three of them hoofed it toward the Denver railroad depot.

"Had to be. The cast-iron strongbox wasn't broken or blown open, it was unlocked. Only a fairly high-level employee of the stageline—or a former employee—would have access to the master key."

"And Leland Langford's convinced that employee is Gil Brennan?"

"Convinced, yeah. Able to prove it, no. Which leaves him neither up the well nor down. It's our job to change all that."

It was not quite 8 A.M. The sun was bright, but the air still cold. Each time a breeze stirred, Joshua could feel it stinging his fresh-shaven cheeks.

Almost a week had passed since Leland had met with Bill. Much of that time was spent tracking down Jimmy, who, Bill finally discovered, was wrangling horses for a cattleman down in the Live Oak country deep in south Texas.

"What about these soldiers?" Jimmy said. "The two sharpshooters. They gonna be on the train with us?"

Bill's eyes watched every doorway, scanned the overhead windows. He shook his head.

"I rode out to Fort Bridger while I was waiting for you," he replied. "I had a parley with this General Durant. He's already sent the soldiers on ahead to Rapid City. That way nobody connects them with us."

"You said this Brennan's pockets are deep," Jimmy reminded him. "Deep enough to corrupt General Durant?"

Hickok considered that one in silence for a minute. In fact, Durant turned out to be one of the few military leaders who disliked Wild Bill. Bill saw more and more of that type out west now as the new "professional officer" class, West Point graduates with little or no battle experience, replaced the Old Corps men like Custer, Sheridan, and Hancock—highly individualistic leaders who had little use for regimental parades and flashy uniforms, men who admired trailblazers like Kit Carson and Davy Crockett and Wild Bill Hickok.

"He's not *our* kind of general, Jimmy," he finally replied. "One of these spit-and-polish fellows who rose through the ranks of the Quartermaster Corps back east. He gave me the usual twaddle-and-bunkum about respect for the chain of command. But my gut hunch tells me he's straight goods. A little stupid, maybe, but honest. On the other hand . . ."

Wild Bill touched the brim of his broad black hat as an elderly lady in a muslin bonnet passed them.

"On the other hand," he continued, "even though he swears by these two soldiers, I don't trust them. Every man has his price."

"Especially enlisted men," Jimmy tossed in.

"A dollar a day don't stretch too far."

Bill nodded. "They might be honest, or they might be sailing under false colors. Don't take your eyes off 'em, James. You either, kid," he added, looking at Joshua. "You toting iron like I told you?"

Joshua nodded. "It's in my underarm holster."

When he had first begun sidekicking with Bill, the famous gunman had given Josh a beautiful old French six-shot pinfire revolver. Taught him to use it, too. That gun had already saved Bill's life.

As for Jimmy, his faded corduroy coat concealed a heavy dragoon pistol. The buckskin sheath he carried in his left hand held a brand-new Winchester '73. A cross-chest bandolier in his poke held a generous supply of two-hundred-grain bullets.

"You best take this rifle for me, Bill," Jimmy suggested. "I been gettin' some stares. White folks get nervous-like when they see us coloreds with guns."

"Let 'em stare," Bill suggested. "I ain't sensitive."

Jimmy was a highly decorated former Union soldier who had served with other black volunteers in the 107th U.S. Colored Troops, the first Negro unit to receive a presidential unit citation for bravery in combat.

Like so many other veterans, black and white, who faced starvation after the war, he had drifted west and become a cowboy for various Texas cattle ranchers. But even with one in

31

every four cowboys now a black man, they were not allowed to bear arms except out on the open range.

The railroad station hove into view, its stones grimed by soot.

"How's your eyes holding up, Jimmy?" Bill inquired. "Still as sharp as when you were a sniper?"

"Sharper," he boasted. "I can still shoot the eyes out of a turkey buzzard at five hundred yards."

"That's good," Bill replied quietly. "Real good. Because mine are failing me, Jimmy. Don't spread that around. I'm going to need yours, old campaigner."

Joshua forgot to breathe, he was so shocked by Bill's admission. Indeed, no greater calamity could afflict a gunman of his legendary stature. The youth had suspected it for some time. Hickok had begun to squint horribly and make obvious excuses why he couldn't see things at long distances.

"How bad, Bill?" Jimmy asked.

"Well, I'm still fine at close range and up into the middle distances. But everything starts to blur at about two hundred yards. Makes me practically useless as a scout. I can cut sign just fine, but I can't read the skyline like I used to."

"And naturally," Jimmy added, not making it a question, "you don't dare wear specs."

Bill snorted. " 'Member what happened to Jack Stubbs when word got out he was wearing specs? It was like throwing a weak buffalo to wolves."

Bill tossed an arm over Joshua's shoulders. "The Philadelphia Kid here has known it for some time. But he's kept it out of his newspaper stories—just about the only thing he *hasn't* mentioned. Thought I didn't know he was protecting me, the little turd."

"What, there's some problem with your eyes?" Josh said with feigned innocence, and all three men laughed.

The northbound 8:15 express arrived right on schedule, venting its boilers in a huge billow of steam. The three men had their tickets punched by an elderly conductor with an ermine-white mustache and a choleric face.

"Sorry, gents—no coloreds allowed in the Pullman cars," he objected as Jimmy started to board. "Third-class coach only."

"He's my servant," Bill explained.

"Yes, sir, but it's rules."

"Even for Wild Bill Hickok?" Jimmy tossed in, and that cinched it. Hickok had spent two years protecting railroad crews from Indians, and was one of the heroes of the railroad men.

"By the Lord Harry, it *is* Wild Bill! Touch you for luck, Bill?"

"My pleasure." Bill gave the man a hearty grip. "No objections to my servant?"

"Objections?" the conductor repeated. "Anybody that doesn't like it can move to another car. All aboard, gentlemen!"

Chapter Four

Wild Bill, Joshua, and Jimmy Davis detrained in Rapid City, Dakota Territory, almost exactly twenty-four hours after boarding in Denver.

After a hearty breakfast of steak and eggs, they reported to the Overland depot in the middle of town. Leland Langford had given them company passes before he left Denver, entitling them to space-available seating on any Overland stagecoach.

"We're meeting Leland at the Martin's Creek way station thirty miles south of town," Bill explained to his friends. "That's where the gold will be loaded and we'll take over the coach."

The next southwest-bound coach was crowded inside, but there was room for three more riders on the box and the top seat behind the driver. The road was deeply rutted and un-

even, but the leather thoroughbraces support-
ing the coach eliminated the rough bouncing
and jostling. Still, Joshua felt himself getting
nauseous, at times, from the rocking and swaying motion, so much like seasickness.

"If you're gonna chuck, kid," Bill warned the
journalist, "stay downwind of me."

This first leg of the trip was fairly populous,
winding past mining camps and homestead
farms, also passing the occasional traveler in
the road. Despite the relative safety, however,
Josh noticed how both Wild Bill and Jimmy
scrutinized everyone, even farmers walking behind their plows.

Three and a half hours after they departed
Rapid City, the coach pulled in at Martin's
Creek Station. The place was laid out more or
less like most of the way stations Josh had seen
since coming west: A low, one-story house of
cottonwood logs chinked with mud served as
dining room and ticket office as well as sleeping
quarters for women, children, and drivers. A
nearby pole corral held the horses that served
as team changes.

A big sod barn behind the corral also doubled
as bunkhouse for the male passengers. It was
common for travelers to show up and sometimes have to wait days for their coach. So the
company supplied a bunk free of charge. Once
passengers purchased their ticket, meals, too,
were provided twice a day.

"Welcome, boys, welcome," Leland greeted
them, leading the new arrivals into the private
office behind the ticket counter and closing the

door. "Thelma will be setting out some eats shortly. Her biscuits are so light, you gotta hold 'em down. You won't be shoving off until tomorrow."

Leland had eyed Jimmy with some reserve at first, not expecting Wild Bill to pick a black man for the shotgun seat. But after Hickok introduced Jimmy as a fellow veteran of the War Between the States, and a sniper in Colonel Augustus Boyd's famous regiment, Leland immediately warmed up to him.

"The soldiers are out in the bunkhouse right now," Leland confided. "A sergeant named John Saville and a corporal named Danny Appling. They seem all right to me. Saville is posing as the Reverend Jerome Peabody, and mister, I mean he looks the part. Appling is posing as a drummer—a toupee seller named Alfred Lawton."

"You been watching them?" Bill asked.

"As best I can. They ain't had no visitors that I've noticed. You'll see both of them when they come in to eat."

"Looks like Overland runs a good operation," Bill complimented him. "Clean stations, animals in good condition, and I see you're moving the mail along 'steada letting it stack up."

"Well, this is the best station because I'm here," Leland admitted. "But things're better, sure. I've got some good division agents now. Under Brennan? Why, Christ! The stations were always filthy, the passengers got nothing but beans and hardtack, and the mail sacks were stacked up to the ceiling."

Bill nodded. "Hell, I remember out in New Mex how some of the drivers would toss full mailbags down over muddy stretches in the trail to get traction. I'd ride the line behind them and find mail left in the mud."

Leland slid open the top drawer of his knee-hole desk.

"Here," he said, tossing Wild Bill a pair of buckskin gloves. "You'll be needing these. Normally the driver would change off at least once between here and Denver. But you'll be pushing the coach all the way through. I notice you've got gambler's hands now."

Bill glanced at the gloves and nodded. "Been so long, I forgot how the reins start to cut after a hundred miles or so."

"You'll also have to use the whip plenty," Leland warned him. "This ain't like the New Mexico Territory you drove. This Black Hills route has plenty of steep grades. Them horses will have to be persuaded now and then."

"Speaking of horses," Bill put in, "I want two extra mounts tied to the rear. Combination horses. With saddle rigs and a sack of grain for 'em."

Leland nodded. "Good idea."

By combination horses Bill meant mounts trained to both traces and saddle riding. That way he and Jimmy would have horses in case they had to give chase to attackers, and extras in case team horses were shot up.

"Where should I ride?" Josh piped up. "In the coach so I can keep an eye on the soldiers?"

37

Bill mulled this a moment, then shook his head.

"I want you in the top seat behind me, Longfellow, keeping an eye on our back trail. I'm not saying Durant's men are bent. But if our soldiers *are* on Gil Brennan's payroll, they won't be able to make their play while we're rolling. Besides, if you want a good story for your newspaper, it'll be topside with us."

Leland stood up and limped to the window beside Bill. He sat on the sill to light his pipe, gazing out toward the barn with a thoughtful frown.

"Bill, there's a lot of people coming and going around these way stations. You remember. Passengers, drivers, stock tenders, drifters on the prod looking for a meal—Brennan is a savvy sonofabitch, and he's not one to do the obvious thing. It ain't just them soldiers you'll need to watch."

Bill's white teeth flashed under his blond mustache. "Don't worry about me, old son. I *always* cut the cards, even if the Pope is dealer."

Harness jangle outside announced the arrival of a coach.

"That's the noon stage to Denver," Leland said. "The one ahead of yours. They'll be laying over until tomorrow morning. C'mon out and stick your feet under the table, boys. Thelma's the best cook on the line."

Joshua trailed out behind his companions, watching the tired passengers file in after washing up outside. They joined others already at the station, swelling the numbers at the long common table to about a dozen.

They made a diverse, democratic group, ranging from the wealthy and well-dressed to poor workers in threadbare clothing. However, one young woman in particular immediately galvanized the attention of every man in the room.

Even at the very first glance, her clothing set her apart. She wore a full skirt with a small waist, scallop-flounced, and a cloak with a sealskin collar. She carried an expensive swansdown muff. Her hands seemed dainty in apple-blossom pink gloves.

Joshua's jaw dropped open in astonished wonder at her beautiful nutshell-shaped eyes the perfect blue of forget-me-nots, the lustrous chestnut hair pulled into a coil on the back of her neck. There was a pearly allure to her skin that even exhaustion couldn't ruin.

"Better pick your eyeballs up off the floor, Longfellow," Wild Bill joked as they scraped back their chairs. "But I can't blame you. She'd make even a gelding feel like a stud."

Wild Bill and Jimmy seemed more interested in taking the measure of the two disguised soldiers. One of the passengers, a coarse and burly man in butternut homespun, frowned when Jimmy took a seat beside Bill.

"I don't eat with niggers," he announced flatly.

"He's a guard on this line, sir," Leland explained politely.

"I don't care if he's Queen Victoria's astrolo-

39

ger," the man shot back. "I don't eat with niggers."

"Sir," said the phony Reverend Peabody, assuming a pious face, "we are all God's children, and all God's children must eat."

"I ain't tryin' to starve him, Reverend, nor beat him or put him back in chains. But I paid good money to ride this line. And I ain't about to eat with niggers."

By now Bill was heaping his plate with mashed potatoes. "Why not?" he asked pleasantly. "After all, *he's* willing to eat with white trash."

"Just keep your nose out of it, pretty boy, or you'll get hurt, and hurt bad."

Bill ignored the threat. "Leland," he said, "if the gent objects so strenuously, then refund his money and let him go eat elsewhere. Or let him fill his plate and eat outside."

"Now, you look here, mister, ain't nobody asked you to stick your nose in the pie."

Bill, like the rest of the men, had removed his hat before he sat down. His long, golden curls covered his collar.

"Well, I'll be damned!" suddenly exclaimed a man at the end of the table. "As I live and breathe, that's Wild Bill Hickok!"

The room went as silent as a classroom after a hard question: Joshua watched the woman, who had haughtily ignored everyone around her, stare at Bill as if he were a dog that had suddenly talked. Bill's gunmetal eyes came up from his plate, coolly meeting those of the man who was complaining.

"Jimmy's with me," he explained with lethal calmness. "As I see it, you have three choices, sir. You can take your refund and leave. You can fix your plate and go eat outside. Or you can shut your stupid cracker mouth right now, and I won't require an apology for your insults to this war hero."

"Bill," Jimmy objected, embarrassed by all this unwanted fuss, "it ain't important. I don't mind eat—"

"If he's good enough to side Wild Bill Hickok," the passenger suddenly relented, "then I guess it's all right."

"*That's* the Christian spirit, sir." The Reverend beamed his benevolence, and Joshua decided John Saville was a good actor indeed.

The tension suddenly broke like a logjam, and the hungry passengers began to make short work of Thelma's excellent grub. All, that is, except the chestnut-haired beauty.

After only a few experimental tastes, she pushed her plate away and stood up.

"Something wrong, ma'am?" the driver asked.

"The food on this line is too salty," she complained. "I don't know how anyone can eat it."

An elderly woman in a calico dress, busy at a sideboard spooning dumplings into a serving bowl, glanced up with an angry frown.

"I been the cook here almost ten years with no complaints, missy," she fumed. "Perhaps it's your *tongue* is too salty."

"In Chicago this food would be fed to hogs at the stockyards." The young woman directed her next question at the driver. "Mr. Donaldson, could you please tell me where the ladies' facilities are located?"

"The ladies' *who*, ma'am?"

Josh noticed that Wild Bill, greatly amused by the turn this trail was taking, had stopped eating. The young woman flushed at all of the attention she was suddenly receiving.

"I mean the place where a lady might . . . might have a private moment, sir."

"A private—? Oh, you mean that nature's calling?"

The driver winked at the man beside him. "Why, there's a hunnert miles of facilities right out back, ma'am. It's called the open prairie. That's what I use."

Thelma grabbed the latest Montgomery Ward catalog off the sideboard. "Take as many pages as you'll need."

The dining room erupted in laughter, and the flustered woman blushed so deeply, even her earlobes turned pink. Joshua, who had already seen where the jakes were out back, rose gallantly to her rescue.

"I can point out the, ahh, facilities to you, ma'am," he volunteered.

The woman glanced at Wild Bill, who was grinning like all the rest. "At least there's *one* gentleman in this room," she bit off angrily, all in a huff.

Donaldson winked again. "Ah-hanh. He just wants to watch you having your 'private moment.' "

"You're *all* vulgar and crude," she charged.

"Well, ain't *she* the prima ballerina?" Thelma remarked as Josh led the offended woman out the side door.

Bill was still grinning when his eyes met those of Corporal Dan Appling, the rabbit-faced soldier disguised as a drummer. So far, following the plan to the letter, Bill had made no contact with either soldier. The man's eyes cut away quickly from Hickok's. Bill had the odd conviction there was guilt in those eyes.

Interesting, he told himself.

Worn down to a frazzle from the train and coach rides, Wild Bill retired early to one of the bedrooms at the back of the station house reserved for drivers. Joshua joined the rest of the male passengers in the bunkhouse at one end of the barn. To avoid any further tension over race mingling, Jimmy selected a clean, dry stall in the barn.

"I'd just as soon sleep with animals anyway," he insisted to Wild Bill. "They got better manners than most people I've met."

Bill's room was basic but clean: an iron bedstead with a feather mattress, a ladder-back chair, a washstand with a metal bowl and pitcher, a few nails driven into the wall for hanging up clothes and gunbelts. The lock was flimsy, so he tilted the chair under the doorknob to reinforce it.

The window, too, bothered him—there was a clear angle of fire toward the bed. So Bill decided to drag the bed to the other wall.

43

That was how he discovered the ingenious death trap.

Bill spotted it the moment he pulled the bedstead away from the wall. A can of blasting powder had been placed under the bed. A short fuse was paid out from the can to a knothole in the room's front wall. It could easily and quickly be lighted from outside.

"Well, God kiss me," Hickok said softly. A lone bead of sweat trickled across his forehead as he realized how close he had come to being blown across the Great Divide.

Leaving the fuse in place, he carefully shook the volatile powder into the metal bowl and poured water on it, neutralizing it. Then he pulled the chair out from under the doorknob and positioned it just to the right of the window. If he pressed one cheek to the wall, Bill could see anyone who came to light the fuse.

He slid each Colt .44 from its holster, palming the wheels to check the loads. Then he watched a copper sunset slowly blaze to darkness behind the hills to the west. Soon Bill realized that clouds had obscured the moon, limiting his vision out the window. He took out his clasp knife and gouged out some of the mud chinking between the logs, giving him a better view of the area near the fuse.

His vigil was long. A stage came in sometime during the night, creating a racket of people and animals out in the yard. Things quieted down eventually; the only sounds were those of a horse occasionally snuffling in the corral or a coyote howling from the distant hills. Dark moon shadows engulfed the yard and buildings. A couple times men sleeping in the barn got up to use the jakes, and Wild Bill listened carefully until they returned to their bunks.

When he caught himself nodding out, Wild Bill resorted to a trick from his days as a military scout. He removed a plug of chewing tobacco from his fob pocket and cut off a sliver with his knife. He cheeked it and got it juicing good, then smeared a little of the juice on the inside of each eyelid. The mild, long-lasting stinging thus produced was adequate to keep him alert.

Perhaps two hours before dawn his vigilance was rewarded. He heard the quiet scuff of boots just beyond the wall. Wild Bill peered through the chink and spotted a shadowy form. A lucifer scraped against something, and sudden flame revealed a beard-stubbled, sharp-featured face.

Wild Bill didn't waste time by sliding the window open. Instead, the glass abruptly shattered as he poked one of his Peacemakers outside.

"Freeze right there, mister!" he barked, his tone brooking no debate.

There was a muttered curse, and the figure turned to run away. Hickok never once hesitated. The Colt jumped in his hand, spitting a line of orange fire. The intruder grunted once, then dropped like a sack of grain.

Jimmy came running out of the barn in his long underwear, levering his Winchester.

"Careful, Jimmy!" Bill called out. "Might be more of 'em out there. And the one I plugged might be a possum player."

45

But Bill's shot had indeed killed the would-be assassin. Leland arrived and ordered the curiosity seekers back to their beds, assuring them the trouble was over. Then he scratched a match to life and squatted on his heels to study the dead man's face.

"It's Race Landrieu," he said immediately. "Used to be the stock tender at Thompson's Canyon Station. One of the men I fired, along with Brennan, when I cleaned house."

Wild Bill nodded, absently thumbing a cartridge into his spent chamber. "Brennan was hoping to nip the problem of Wild Bill Hickok in the bud early on. Figured the gold would then be easier pickings."

"Christ," Leland swore. "Well, he figured it wrong."

Joshua, still tucking in his shirttail, had joined them in time to hear Bill explain about the blasting powder. "But how could Brennan have known, so soon, that you were on this case, Bill? It's supposed to be a secret."

"He's got informers, that's how. And I'm guessing word came from within General Durant's command structure."

"The soldiers out in the bunkhouse, you mean?"

Hickok shrugged. "What's after what's next? Damned if I know. But they were out here early enough."

"I better get somebody to bury him," Leland said, still staring at the corpse.

"Nix on that," Bill told him. "You said you

want to send a message to Brennan and his gun-throwers, right?"

"Right as rain."

"All right, then. That's what we're going to do. This fight ain't going to be pretty, Leland. This here tonight is just the opening volley. Now, here's what I want you to do. . . ."

Chapter Five

The next morning a shocking sight greeted the waking passengers at Martin's Creek Station: Race Landrieu's body hung from the limbs of a massive white oak beside the pole corral. A sign had been pinned to his shirt: GIL BRENNAN'S FAVORITE BOY.

Wild Bill, Joshua, Jimmy Davis, and Leland Langford sat down to breakfast before the rest had risen.

Joshua, still taken aback at the sight out in the yard, aimed a questioning glance at his hero. Wild Bill Hickok had always been a hard man when the situation required it, and he was not afraid to put the noose before the gavel. After all, it was he who had coined the phrase "shoot first and ask questions later." But this display outside was blatant vigilantiism pure and simple.

"How long will the body hang there?" Josh asked.

Hickok, busy enjoying Thelma's delicious grits, didn't even look up from his plate. "That's Leland's call. Personally, I'd leave it up until the stink gets too raw. Brennan's minions will see it, and word will spread."

"It'll stay up there at least all day today," Leland said. "Around here, news travels faster than spit through a trumpet. I agree with Bill. It seems cruel, maybe, but I know Gil Brennan. If you mean to whip him and his bunch, rearguard actions won't get it done. Let them see what they're up against."

"What time are we scheduled to pull out?" Bill asked Leland, sopping a biscuit in gravy.

"Late morning, J. B. One Denver coach will roll out at eight A.M. We'll be hitching your stage up inside the barn. Both soldiers will report to you there."

Wild Bill nodded. "Speaking of the soldiers," he said to Joshua, "you keep an eye on 'em last night?"

Josh nodded. "They didn't do anything that looked suspicious to me. The one disguised as a preacher is *good*. He sure sounds like a genuine man of God."

Wild Bill snorted at that one. "Even the devil can cite Scripture. Keep watching them."

By now the others were up and filing inside to eat. Thelma was still serving up plates of eggs, ham, and grits when the haughty beauty who had insulted her cooking yesterday stormed into the room, her eyes flashing fire.

"*You!*" she exclaimed, marching right up to Bill's chair. "Are you responsible for that barbarism outside?"

Bill took her in with an amused glance. Her gentle, pleasing brow seemed wildly at odds with angry eyes like molten metal.

"Well now, miss," he replied calmly, "I'd say the dead man was responsible for it. A man tries to blow me into little bits, I tend to resent it—I'm funny that way."

"So it was you?"

"That ordered him put on display? Guilty as charged, and unrepentant."

"You . . . this . . . Surely to God you can't be serious, Mr. Hickok? This isn't Christian!"

"That dog won't hunt. What you mean is it ain't New Testament. But it's Old Testament. And last I heard, both are still part of the Bible."

Now that her first shock had passed, a visible storm of anger rose inside her. She turned to the man she thought was a preacher, who had just filed in with the rest.

"Tell him, Reverend Peabody. Tell him he's wrong."

Sergeant Saville, too, looked shaken. But he shook his head. "I'm sorry, Charlene. Mr. Hickok may not be a theologian, but he is correct. Remember, too, there's no U.S. marshal out here, so the area is essentially required to resort to vigilante law."

" 'Preciate that, Rev," Bill told him.

Frustrated but not daunted, Charlene stood her ground. "My father will hear of this, Mr. Hickok."

"And just who might your sire be?"

"General Stanley Durant, commanding officer of Fort Bridger down near Denver. I've come out to live with him, and I *will* report this . . . this barbaric act!"

A grin divided Hickok's handsome face. He looked at Leland. "Can you believe this little spitfire came out of the loins of Old Sobersides? Maybe there was a sergeant hiding in the woodpile?"

Red splotches of anger leaped into her cheeks. She slapped Bill hard, a stinging blow that made Joshua wince.

"Strong arm, too," Bill added as her hand print glowed red on his face, and the rest laughed at his clowning. "Even with your nose out of joint, Miss Durant, you're a looker."

More laughter bubbled through the room, and she stormed toward the door, her bustled skirts swishing.

"I'll be waiting in the coach, Mr. Donaldson," she informed her driver, biting off the words in anger. "I sorely regret not waiting for space on a train. I'd rather starve than be in the same room with that beast."

But she couldn't resist one last barb. She turned from the doorway to stare at Wild Bill with those forget-me-not eyes.

"The famous Wild Bill Hickok," she said scornfully. "He walks with kings but never loses the *common* touch. As in common criminal."

"She's headstrong, that one," Bill told Leland after she stormed off. "I'm glad she ain't my problem. I'd rather take my chances with a sore-tailed bear than a firebrand like that."

Charlene Durant's coach rolled out at 8 A.M., so crowded that even the top seat was occupied. With Bill and Jimmy keeping watch in the yard, Winchesters ready, Leland and his stock tender transferred the gold bars from the safe inside the station house to the strongbox inside the coach.

"This is one of the new Wells Fargo strongboxes, with a combination lock instead of a key," Leland explained. "Last heist, the strongbox was opened with a key. Brennan must have copied Overland's before I fired him."

Wild Bill nodded. "Sure, nothing to it. You just press the key into soap or wax to get the impression. Hell, if you've got a lead ladle, there's your copy."

Bill leaned back out of the Concord coach and looked at Josh.

"Run get the soldiers and send them here to see me," he told the youth. After Josh had left the big sod barn, Bill looked at Jimmy.

"From here on out," he told his shotgun rider, "don't let either one of those soldiers behind you unless I've got you backed. For aught I know, they're both honest men. But neither one of us gets careless, hear?"

"Hell, Bill, you're preaching to the choir. I don't even trust you."

Hickok laughed. "That's why I looked you up, Jimmy."

John Saville and Dan Appling stepped inside from the bright sunlight, squinting in the dimness.

"Howdy, boys," Bill greeted them. He transferred his Winchester to his left hand and shook both their hands. "I'm J. B. Hickok. My friend here is Jimmy Davis. He'll be roosting on the hot seat. He fought his way into Secessia with the 107th, chased Bobby Lee himself out of his bathtub. I take it General Durant has fully briefed you?"

"Yessir," Sergeant Saville replied. "Only, I'm starting to warm up to this preacher disguise. I may turn the other cheek when the lead starts flying."

All four men laughed. Hell, he seems all right, Bill thought. But Rabbit-Face there has trouble meeting my eye. Still, that doesn't prove anything. Maybe he feared the Evil Eye.

"You boys carrying the Smith and Wesson Cavalry issue?"

Saville nodded. "With fifty rounds each in our pokes."

"But none of them fancy bandoliers like Jimmy's got," Appling tossed in.

"I want you boys on opposite sides of the coach at all times. But remember, you're vulnerable to snipers if you sit too far forward, in front of the windows."

"Best to keep the dust shades down at least partway," Leland suggested.

"We *won't* try to outrun the trouble," Bill

warned them, "except snipers. If we're jumped, we're taking it by the horns. That means I halt the coach immediately and you two dive out if you can. You know how to tuck and roll under fire—cover down as soon as you can, then find your targets. Shoot to kill."

"Only way we know how," Saville affirmed.

"You're pulling out in about one hour," Leland informed them. "Thelma's got lunch ready now. Eat hearty—it's your last good meal on this line. From now on, it's bean soup and cornbread. We've had trouble keeping cooks at the other way stations. Cattle outfits steal them from us at double our wages."

"Friend, we're grateful for God's bounty," Saville said piously, playing Reverend Peabody to the hilt. Again they all laughed.

"What do you think, J. B.?" Leland demanded as soon as the soldiers left the barn.

"Well, I thought Saville pushed it one time too many with mocking his disguise. But if I was gambling on odds, I'd wager they're straight-arrow," he replied. "Still, I like Jimmy's attitude—don't trust anybody."

"Go up to the station and eat," Leland told them. "I'll hitch the team to the traces. Pick your two cavvy horses out of the corral. I recommend that sorrel with the white boots and the lineback dun. They've both got good bottom and they're bullet-wise. I'll lash saddles and bridles behind the top seat."

Bill nodded. Halfway across the yard, he paused to stare at the dead man swaying in the breeze. Bluebottle flies covered Race Landrieu's face like a moving black mask.

"From what Leland says," Jimmy observed beside him, "that won't scare Gil Brennan. It'll just put more fight into him."

"Brennan doesn't do the dirt work," Bill reminded him. "It'll scare somebody."

"You know," Jimmy confessed as they resumed walking. "After what we seen in the war? That doesn't even turn my stomach. Hell, I'm hungry as four men."

"I know." Bill grinned again. "Like I said, Jimmy—that's why I looked you up. I got a hunch we're going to *need* strong stomachs before this is over. Now let's go eat."

Chapter Six

Rick Collins's blunt, pockmarked face wrinkled like a rubber mask when he frowned. He watched Sandy Urbanski carefully use strong sinew thread to tie a small rawhide pouch to a flaked-flint arrow point.

"The hell you doing?" he demanded.

Sandy's hard-bitten eyes never once looked up from his task. He sat at a crude plank table, working in the light of an old skunk-oil lamp. His chair was an empty nail keg. Flattened bean cans had been used to patch the decrepit walls of the old prospector's shack where the two men stayed when working a job for Gil Brennan.

"It's a little trick I learnt from a Yaqui down in Sonora," Sandy muttered in reply. "It's called an explosive arrow. There!"

Sandy grinned when he had the pouch tied down just right.

"Mister God Almighty Hickok thought he was pretty smart when he strung Race up like a side of beef," Sandy told his partner. "Figured we'd take one look and run like a river when the snow melts. But Hickok figured it wrong."

Sandy set the explosive arrow beside four others he'd already finished. He started in on number six.

"Each pouch," he explained, "is filt with nitro-laced blasting powder. There's also a percussion cap, stuck between the powder and one edge of the arrow point. The point strikes the target hard, the impact detonates the cap, the cap explodes the powder."

"Don'cha have to get too close to make them caps go off?"

"Shoo, not with my crossbow," Sandy assured him. "It's got twice the throwin' power of any Comanche osage bow I ever did see, tell you that. And I seen Yaquis hurl 'em seven, eight hunnert yards at Mexican lancers. Scared the Jesus out of 'em, too. The arrows what missed men started fires in the cassions and supply wagons. And I seen one even exploded a powder limber. Blew half a squad to hell on the spot."

Sandy speared his fingers through his thick dark hair, pushing the bulk of it back to clear his vision for the task. "But it's what they do to a *man* that sets you back on your heels. I seen it, Rick, oh man I seen it. A crossbow makes the point hit so hard, the cap don't even need to strike bone. The point makes just its usual-size hole going in. But by the time it explodes and comes out?"

Sandy looked up, making a pulpit pause to build the drama.

"Yeah, what then?" Collins demanded.

"Why, mister, it makes a hole big as a green apple. Hell, even if you hit an arm or a leg, your target will die quick from shock or blood loss. And if you hit the head, why, that's a sockdollager. Blows one side off like a melon under a train wheel."

Sandy laughed at the thought of it. In the lamplight the knife scar under his left eye seemed to shine like a wet white worm.

"Wild Bill Hickok won't be so prettified with half his face missing. But we'll be needing the other half to claim that reward in Texas."

"But you know Brennan has got this other plan, the one where—"

"Brennan ain't so permanent, if you take my drift? 'Sides, we ain't ignoring his fancy-dan diversion plan. This here plan of mine is just an extra try, is all. Gil ain't partic'lar whose plan it is, long as we get the swag."

"I guess that's so. When we gonna jump 'em?"

"Late this afternoon," Sandy replied. "I got it figured. They'll pull into Schofield Station around three o'clock. About five miles out of Schofield, the trail winds a whole bunch to avoid landslide slopes. That'll slow 'em down. Then we'll—"

Sandy hesitated when he heard his blood bay gelding whinny softly outside.

"It's just a raccoon that got too close," Collins explained, glancing out the open door.

Sandy believed him. But he waited at least ten seconds anyway, knowing the horse would whinny again if there was man trouble. It stayed quiet, and he resumed his explanation.

"We'll take up good positions on Bodmer's Ridge. I'll use my crossbow on Hickok, you'll air out the darky and the kid with my Yellow Boy. Hell, even if one or both of us misses, which ain't too likely, they'll be rattled bad. Them soldiers might be able to hang out a window and pop 'em at close range. They practiced it a little before Hickok got out here."

Rick frowned at that. "Yeah, well, then they might try to lay claim to the reward on Hickok," he complained.

"Much like a castrated bull, you just don't get it, do you? These soldiers is still in the Army, remember? Might be hard to explain to a court-martial board why they're traipsing off to Texas with Bill Hickok's severed head in a sack."

Sandy brandished one of the arrows. "And why do you think I'm making these cannon-ball arrows? One of these little pups hits him, there won't be no discussion over who done it."

Reward money wasn't really Sandy's chief consideration. After all, his share of the previous gold heists had already made him a rich man, even after Brennan had to split it so many ways. But money was gone once you spent it; fame, in contrast, belonged to a man even after death. And the man who sent the "unkillable" Wild Bill Hickok to his grave was assured a spot in history. A tarnished spot, to be sure, but a spot nonetheless.

"There," Sandy announced as he finished rigging the sixth explosive arrow. "Here, Ricky, take these real careful-like and slant 'em against the wall."

Collins had no trouble with the arrows. But he clumsily knocked against the brass-framed Winchester Yellow Boy that was propped up against the nearest wall. It slid fast and hit the rammed-earth floor, its stock banging hard.

"Christ! Take care, you soft-brained fool! I still ain't fixed that worn sear. That rifle's hair-trigger until I fix it. You'll have to handle it easy."

Sandy had retained one of the arrows, cocking his crossbow and loading the arrow to make sure it still fit the aiming groove.

"Snug as a virgin on her wedding night," he pronounced, his voice smug with satisfaction. "Let's grab leather, Ricky. I want plenty of time to take up a good position. It ain't every day a man gets a crack at a 'living legend.'"

Just past forenoon Wild Bill kicked off the brake, cracked his blacksnake over the team, and the journey southwest to Denver was under way.

The first stretch of trail, between Martin's Creek and Schofield Station in Wyoming, was easy to defend against. Slightly rolling prairie stretched out on both sides, grassy but treeless, providing little opportunity for dry-gulchers. But Wild Bill had already warned everyone to maintain maximum vigilance every foot of the way.

They remained especially wary when they met any traffic coming from the opposite direction. But they passed only one lone horseman, a sodbuster on a big gray dray horse, and a hardware drummer driving a light van wagon. Both men called out cheery greetings.

"Cover those doors," Bill ordered Jimmy, meaning the double rear doors of the van. Jimmy thumbed his rifle to full cock as the van rolled past them, slewing around on the box until the vehicle had rattled out of sight. Then he eased the hammer back down to half cock.

"You want me to search the jackrabbits and prairie dogs, too?" Joshua joked from the top seat behind them, where he rode like a swaying sailor in the crow's nest.

"Kid," Bill replied, "when you've been jumped as much as I have, you start looking behind the clouds, even. I'd rather be called a nervous Nellie than 'the dearly departed.'"

Jimmy laid his Winchester across his thighs and took out the makings. Bending against the breeze, he shaped himself a smoke.

"Bill's right," he said as he licked the paper and quirled the ends. "Very few men die when they expect to. Death ain't one for making appointments."

"Speaking of which," Hickok told Joshua, "I want you glancing often down both sides of the coach—you take my drift?"

The reporter nodded. Bill didn't want any guns showing from inside. The soldiers had not made him suspicious; he just refused to assume anything.

Perhaps twenty miles out of Martin's Creek Station a cloudburst opened up overhead. Josh dug out their oilcloth rain slickers.

"Hope it don't turn into a gully-washer," Hickok fretted, slanting his hat so the water ran off better. "If mud clumps to those wheels, we'll have to stop and scrape 'em. Course, that's better than what always happened to me out in New Mex Territory. Out there, the wood got so consarned dry and was always shrinking the wheels. Then they pop right out of the iron rims."

But the rainstorm blew off to the north, over the main body of the Black Hills, and a warm September sun reappeared in a sky of deep, bottomless blue.

A few miles before Schofield Station the terrain began to change again, more trees appearing. Bill reined in the team, a frown firming his features.

" 'S'matter?" Jimmy demanded, bringing his rifle up to the low port, ready.

"Sit tight, boys," Wild Bill called down to the soldiers. "I'm just playing it safe against snipers."

Wild Bill nodded at a thick stand of willows and scrub oaks crowding the trail on Jimmy's side. He let the horses set their own slow pace.

"Now, that ain't the best ambush point," he told Joshua and Jimmy. "I'd stay farther back if I was a sharpshooter looking for quick kills at low risk. But for that very reason, we best respect it. Evidently, Brennan's bunch ain't one to do the obvious thing. Joshua."

"What?"

"Quit scribbling in that pad and crawl back over the boot. Watch them two horses, especially the sorrel. While you're at it, break out your shooter. Let me know if their ears prick. Jimmy, get flat and watch them trees."

Bill shucked out a Peacemaker in his right hand, holding the reins loosely in his left. But the coach eased by without incident.

"Don't forget, Jimmy," Bill said as he whipped the team up to a trot. "I need your eyes on the horizons. Mine fade on me at them distances."

They rolled into the next way station, where the stock tender was waiting to unhitch the team so they could drink from the stone trough in the yard. He also gave them a quick rubdown with old grain sacks—this team would not be changed until they stopped for the night at the next station.

The soldiers climbed out and headed for the jakes out back.

"Take care of our saddle band," Wild Bill told Joshua. "The stock tender's got his hands full with the team. And while you're out here, keep a weather eye out for trouble. Keep that coach in sight."

There was a water casket outside the door of the station house. Wild Bill lifted the top off and let it dangle by its rope tether while he dipped out a drink.

"—this is *outrageous!*" complained a familiar

female voice from inside. "What authority does the driver have to put a passenger off his coach? I did nothing wrong! All I did was remind him to watch his language in front of ladies."

Bill's eyes met Jimmy's, and both men grinned.

"A bad penny always turns up," Bill quipped. "Looks like Donaldson finally took mercy on the rest of his passengers."

"Lord, ain't *she* the mother of the Devil?" Jimmy said. "I don't know if I got the stones to go in there, Bill."

"Buck up, old son. Whatever don't kill you can only leave you stronger."

Both men stepped inside and swept off their hats. Charlene Durant ignored them, for she had cornered the agent, a paunchy, middle-aged man who looked almost terrified, to give him a ration of her ire. Today she wore a blue cotton skirt with a crisp white shirtwaist, her chestnut hair in two thick, shining plaits.

"My father will be fully apprised of this outrage," she fumed. "I had no idea the West was populated by two-legged beasts!"

This station was equipped with a short plank bar and a small selection of liquor on two wall shelves behind it. The bartender doubled as the cook. He had flattened out a pan of dough and was cutting biscuit rounds with a tin cup. The two new arrivals bellied up to the bar, placing their elbows carefully to avoid the beer spills.

"Name your pizen, gents."

"Two bourbons with a beer posse," Wild Bill

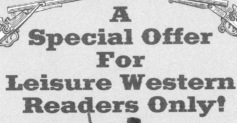

GET YOUR 4
FREE* BOOKS NOW—
A VALUE BETWEEN
$16 AND $20

Mail the Free* Book Certificate Today!

FREE* BOOKS
CERTIFICATE!

YES! I want to subscribe to the Leisure Western Book Club. Please send me my 4 FREE* BOOKS. Then, each month, I'll receive the four newest Leisure Western Selections to preview FREE* for 10 days. If I decide to keep them, I will pay the Special Member's Only discounted price of just $3.36 each, a total of $13.44 ($14.50 US in Canada). This saves me between $3 and $6 off the bookstore price. There are no shipping, handling or other charges.* There is no minimum number of books I must buy and I may cancel the program at any time. In any case, the 4 FREE* BOOKS are mine to keep—at a value of between $17 and $20!

*In Canada, add $5.00 Canadian shipping and handling per order for first shipment. For all subsequent shipments to Canada the cost of membership in the Book Club is $14.50 US, which includes $7.50 shipping and handling per month. All payments must be made in US currency.

Name _____

Address _____

City _____ State _____ Country _____

Zip _____ Telephone _____

Tear here and mail your FREE* book card today!

Get Four Books Totally
F R E E* –
A Value between
$16 and $20

Tear here and mail your FREE* book card today!

PLEASE RUSH
MY FOUR FREE*
BOOKS TO ME
RIGHT AWAY!

LeisureWestern Book Club
P.O. Box 6613
Edison, NJ 08818-6613

said, flipping a silver dollar onto the bar. "Bar could use a quick wipe, too."

"Sorry, fellows," he said, drying it with a dirty apron.

"Stand by for the blast," Jimmy muttered. "Here comes our hellcat, and her claws are out."

"Mr. Hickok," she said, "are you driving that stage outside?"

Her imperious assumption that she had a right to demand this made Bill grin at her.

"Well, now, Miss Durant, I can't hardly drive it *in*side, now can I?"

The bardog and Jimmy both sniggered while Charlene Durant flushed red as seep clay.

"Mr. Hickok," she tried again, her tone less demanding, "will you *please* help me get out of this flea pit? I was left behind simply because *I* asked the driver to stop cussing so much—and so profanely."

"If it ain't profane, than what use is cussing? Anyhow, we're filled up, ma'am."

"Filled—?" She glanced around the nearly empty station. All she saw were the two men at the bar and the preacher and the salesman, who had just come inside. She glanced out the windows and saw empty yard. "But then, where are the rest of your passengers?"

Wild Bill picked up his shot glass between thumb and forefinger and saw his own eye looking back at him in the golden reflection. He tossed back the bourbon, then used his neckerchief to fastidiously wipe off his mustache.

"What I mean, Miss Durant, is that our coach can't take on any more passengers."

"But why?"

Bill quaffed half of his beer and again wiped his mustache. "You sure ask a lot of questions. Well, for starters, because you slapped my face back at Martin's Creek. I've been told that it's quite handsome. I'm protective of it, and if you were a man I could have hit you. It's easy to hit somebody you know won't hit you back."

"Well, go ahead and hit back."

His eyes narrowed. "That option's open."

"Your handsome face! You insufferable egotist."

Bill pushed away from the bar and picked up his hat, slapping the dust out of it. "That's another reason why we're full up. I don't like your tart mouth, m'heart. Your tongue's been soaking in brine."

She was getting more desperate as the men prepared to leave.

"*Please*, Mr. Hickok? Please don't leave me stranded here? I'm . . . I'm sorry I insulted you. And . . . hit you."

"And ain't it a handsome face?"

She frowned, but relented. "It's quite handsome, and you know it. I've seen few that are finer."

He, too, frowned. "But you're saying you've seen finer?"

"Mr. Hickok, please! May I ride with you?"

Bill blew his cheeks out, then gave a fluttering sigh. "Flattery works with us egotists. Yeah, you can ride along. But only on one condition."

His tone made her pale slightly. "A . . . condition? What might that be?"

Bill looked at Jimmy, and they both laughed.

"Not what you're thinking, city girl. I want you to promise that, at the first sign of any trouble, you'll get down onto the floor of the coach and *stay* there."

"Then—you're expecting trouble?"

"As you prove, it tends to find me, yes. All funning aside, it could get very dangerous. You're sure you can't wait here a day?"

She cast a woebegone glance around the dingy station. "Yes, I'm absolutely certain. And yes, I will do as you request—I appreciate your taking me along."

She spoke quite graciously, and Bill had to admire her charm. He slanted a glance at John Saville. "How 'bout you, Reverend Peabody? Any objection if this young lady rides with you and Mr. Lawton?"

"All God's children are welcome, Mr. Hickok."

"Amen, brother." Bill's eyes traveled the length of her shapely figure. "That's mighty Christian of you, Rev. Maybe you can even teach her a little humility, too."

"Why, you can just—" She caught herself just in time. "I'll get my valise," she said archly, turning away with the grace of a ballerina on her pointes.

"You sure this is wise, Bill?" Jimmy asked as they headed back outside.

"The last 'wise' thing I did, Jimmy, was fold on aces and eights against a full house. Hell, I warned the little spitfire. If she gets herself shot up, it ain't our funeral."

67

The coach waited out in the yard, the team hitched again. The stock tender was greasing the axles.

"The country changes up ahead," Bill warned Jimmy. "Ridges and rock nests. Keep your eyes peeled. Now we start earning our pay."

Chapter Seven

"A stage driver," Wild Bill told Jimmy and Joshua, "earns just enough to keep the wolf from the door. Yet, it's one of the most dangerous jobs in the West. Low pay, high risk—just like being a lawman in a cowtown. He-*yah*!" he shouted, cracking his blacksnake to coax the team up a long incline.

A late-afternoon sun was losing its warmth and casting long, slanting shadows over the denuded hills surrounding them. This area had been stripped of trees to provide timber supports for the mining industry.

Even though Wild Bill's eyes no longer picked up details at long distance, he could still easily read the terrain. And he didn't like what he was reading now.

"Jimmy?"

"Yo!"

"My old scouting bones tell me that low ridge off to our left is trouble. Is it within rifle range, you think?"

The sharpshooter nodded. "Easy. 'Bout five, six hundred yards, Bill."

"That's beyond most men's effective range. But not trained snipers."

"I could make it easy," Jimmy affirmed. "Almost twice that, even, if I had my old Big Fifty."

"Kid," Bill called up to Josh, "flatten down again. And hold on. We'll be putting on some speed."

Jimmy prepared by checking his rear sight and raising it a little to adjust for windage at that distance.

"If they start plinking at us," Hickok told him, "I won't be useful for making out any muzzle flash or smoke. Try to locate it, Jimmy. Now, hang on."

Bill turned his head to the left and shouted below: "We're picking up the pace for a stretch, folks! Keep away from the windows, especially on the driver's side."

This team had now been in the traces since morning. But they were well-grained and watered, and the pace had not been too grueling. Experience told Bill they still had plenty of bottom. He laid to the whip, relying on the noise to chuck them up to a strong run.

"Gee up! He-*yah!* Hee-*YAH!*"

Joshua, facedown behind the top seat, held on to the running rails for dear life. He was surprised at finding out just how fast a stagecoach could get rolling, and what an infernal racket it made at top speed. The jangle and clatter of traces and tug chains, the thunder of iron-shod hooves, the splitting crack of the whip as well as Bill's full-throated shouts—it all made talking impossible, not that he had anything to say. Not with this huge lump of fear in his throat.

There was also the powerful rocking and swaying of the braced coach—he had the eerie sensation that he was adrift on a raft in a storm-tossed sea.

They were perhaps halfway past the low ridge when Joshua decided that, once again, Wild Bill was playing it too safe—Just as he had done earlier at the stand of willows. Maybe Bill was getting more edgy because—

Thwap!

An entire corner of the box, only inches from Wild Bill's left thigh, literally exploded in shards and splinters of burning wood. One splinter flew back and pierced Joshua's right cheek.

Thwap!

More shards and splinters sprayed Wild Bill and Joshua. But there was no sound of gunfire. God Almighty, the journalist thought as he fought down a welling of panic. Was somebody firing small artillery shells?

Then Josh spotted an arrow buried in the box. At the same time, the first sounds of a rifle firing reached Josh's ears. He looked up quickly and thought he glimpsed a brief spark of muzzle fire.

Evidently Jimmy had spotted it too. The fearless shotgun rider, ignoring his own risk, went

71

up into a dangerously exposed kneeling-offhand position. He began levering and firing, levering and firing, keeping it hot for the gunners on the ridge.

Warm brass casings glinted in the sunlight as they were ejected, clattering and rolling all around Josh's head. Apparently Jimmy's shots were having some effect—no more bullets or those god-awful arrows were striking the coach. But Wild Bill was again taking no chances—not until the ridge faded behind them did he slow his merciless whipping of the team.

"I think we're out of their trap," he told the others as he reined in the exhausted team behind a protective knoll.

"All right down below?" he called over his shoulder.

"We're all fine," Saville's voice replied. "Although Miss Durant looks a bit peaked."

Wild Bill was already calm enough to grin at that.

"Damn, Bill, you called it like a gang boss," Jimmy admired, already thumbing reloads into his repeater. "If you hadn't whipped the team up, all three of us might be looking up to see daisies."

Bill glanced back at Josh. "Christ! You hit, kid?"

Josh felt the blood running down his cheek. But the wound wasn't deep. "Nah. Just a splinter."

"Wash it with calomel," Bill suggested. "There's some in my bedroll."

But Josh wanted answers. "What in Sam Hill

were those first shots, Bill? Look! They blew fist-sized chunks out of the wood. It's still smoldering."

"Exploding arrows," Bill replied tersely. "I'll explain later, Longfellow. Right now I got to go calling."

Hickok was peeling off his duster as he spoke. Josh watched him quickly buckle on his spurs of fancy Mexican silver. He tossed his gloves and the reins to Jimmy, laid the whip on the box.

"After I ride out, keep the coach rolling at a walk until the team's done blowing. Then hold 'em at an easy trot again. We need to make the next way station before it gets too dark. I'll meet you on ahead."

Wild Bill looked at Joshua. "Your nerves look steady. Wash that cut out, then c'mon down on the box and take Jimmy's long gun. You'll ride the hot seat until I get back."

Joshua's reporter instincts made him eager to fire off more questions. But Wild Bill had already leaped down off the box and moved behind the coach.

"Toss down one of the saddles and bridles," he called up. "Don't hit me with the damn thing."

While Joshua unlashed one of the narrow-cantled cowboy saddles, Wild Bill untied the sorrel from behind the coach. The sorrel had taken to Bill instantly back at Martin's Creek Station, and now it bumped its nose against his chest in greeting.

Hickok efficiently and quickly rigged the animal and cinched the girth, then checked the latigos. The stirrups needed adjusting for his legs, but they'd have to do.

This saddle had no scabbard, so he secured his Winchester with the cantle straps. He stepped up into leather, reined the sorrel around toward the ridge, and tickled its flank with a spur. The gelding responded instantly, quickly reaching a strong gallop.

Wild Bill knew he couldn't risk directly approaching the ridge—his eyes wouldn't allow it. But he had spotted a series of low draws and dry washes that should provide cover in case the ambushers were still on the ridge. He reined the sorrel down to an easy lope and entered the first draw.

A few times the ground leveled, exposing him briefly, and Bill borrowed a defensive riding posture he'd learned from fighting Sioux and Cheyennes. He slid off to the right side of the horse, gripping it high around the neck with its body between him and the ridge.

Only about ten minutes after he'd ridden out, Hickok rounded the end of a rocky spur and spotted them: two riders retreating at an unhurried pace, obviously not expecting trouble.

"My eyes are weak," he told the sorrel as he swung down, landing cat-footed, "but we'll give 'em a little kiss so they know we're thinking of 'em."

He ground-hitched his mount, then quickly untied his rifle. Bill knew he couldn't assure hits on the men, and he usually tried to avoid shooting horses. But Leland and the U.S. government had requested gun law. And as those exploding arrows proved, Gil Brennan's hardcases played rough and dirty. It was important to get on their nerves early and answer blow for blow.

He dropped into a prone position among a scattering of boulders and laid a bead on one of the horses. The brass butt-plate of his Winchester kicked against his shoulder, kicked again, and both horses went down. Bill's lightly oiled mechanism snicked flawlessly as brass casings rattled against the rocks, the sharp cracks of the '73 echoing out across the open terrain in a series of rapidly diminishing *chuff* sounds.

The surprised dry-gulchers were more interested in taking cover than in firing back. But Wild Bill's vision was at the limit of its dependable range now—a fact that frustrated him greatly despite his legendary aplomb.

"A couple years ago," he almost apologized to the sorrel, "I could have wiped both those snakes out of the saddle instead of punishing their horses. I ain't bragging this mission—it's damned humiliating is what it is. I've about had my belly full of Gil Brennan and his Bowery thugs. Let's vamoose, boy."

Chapter Eight

Charlene Durant rued the day she had ever agreed to join her father at Fort Bridger. And she *especially* regretted her decision to come west by stagecoach. After four years of boarding school in Chicago, the prospect had seemed like a wonderful adventure.

Instead, it had become one long nightmare. Worse than a nightmare, actually, because it didn't end when she opened her eyes. She had expected to find a rustic but romantic civilization out here; instead, there were nothing but boorish, vulgar men and coarse women with leathery skin.

The sun had set long ago, but generous moonwash illuminated the interior of the Concord coach. She watched as the toupee salesman, Alfred Lawton, once again slid the slim silver flask out of his inside jacket pocket. He had been drinking for the past two hours, and now he looked at her with a suggestive leer.

"Sure you won't have a drink, miss?" he slurred. "Does wonders for the boredom."

"No, thank you," she practically snapped. Although she had indeed been tempted to accept a drink hours earlier, when all that shooting erupted.

She felt tired from her eyes to her insteps. Never again would she travel by one of these infernal conveyances. How did people endure it? She had been unable to eat the slop they called food, and by now her stomach was pinched from hunger. And despite the evening chill outside, her face felt hot and sticky. Oh, how she wished she could wash it with a cool cloth.

Reverend Peabody's knee once again "accidentally" bumped hers, and she jerked back from the unwelcome contact. Both of these men were getting on her nerves. Even the preacher—for a man of God, he seemed to have a worldly fascination with staring at her bosom. And both men had a musty, unwashed-animal smell that forced her to breathe through her mouth.

Indeed, the three men outside were among the only halfway-clean specimens she'd seen since crossing the Mississippi River. The young reporter, Joshua, was most definitely a gentleman, although no doubt learning coarse habits from the company he kept. So, too, was the Negro guard, although, like Wild Bill, he had the haunting eyes of men who had seen ugly things

in their time. However, Hickok obviously val-
ued good cloth and excellent tailoring.

"Yard lamps up ahead," Lawton reported,
hanging his head out one of the windows.
"Looks like we're finally pulling in to a way station."

"Thank God," Charlene couldn't help saying
as relief flooded through her.

"Yes, the Lord provides," Peabody intoned
solemnly.

But once again Charlene detected an almost
ironic thread in his tone. And again, after he
spoke, his eyes seemed to send an unspoken sig-
nal to Lawton—as if they were sharing a joke
between them. She also noticed that both men
carried revolvers under their coats. They had
pulled them out during all the commotion, and
even the Reverend seemed eager to use his.

She was too tired, however, to care much
about anything but the prospect of a hot bath
and—she hoped—clean bed linens. The stage
swung into the station yard, and she read the
sign with gilded wooden letters that extended
over the front door: THOMPSON'S CANYON STA-
TION.

The conveyance rocked to a stop and Reverend Peabody leaped out first, lowering the iron
step for her and handing her down. She could
feel that her clothes needed "a good pull-down"
as her long-departed mother used to say. But
Charlene felt too tired to bother.

"You'll feel better after a good night's rest,"
the Reverend assured her, removing his hand
from her arm much later than he needed to.

But again his eyes sent some secret message to Lawton, and Charlene felt a vague stirring of apprehension.

Wild Bill climbed down off the box, weary and sleepy, his throat scratchy from trail dust. He hung back from the others, watching while a young Mexican boy drove the stage into the barn and began unhitching the team.

Leland had warned Bill that, even after cleaning house at Overland, he couldn't guarantee the honesty of all the new workers. But Hickok was not unduly worried about the gold being secretly seized at layovers. The new combination-lock strongbox was bolted to the floor of the coach, and it required a special tool only the Denver Mint possessed to remove it—that or an explosive charge.

Hickok waved off the stock tender and took care of the two-horse saddle band himself. He curried off the dried sweat and rubbed them down, then turned them out into the paddock after hanging nose bags of crushed barley on them.

All of the extra work was really just to get the lay of the place. Race Landrieu, the man he had killed back at Martin's Creek, had worked here before Leland cashiered him. For no specific reason, that made Bill want to look around.

He ducked under the tie rail out front, grunting wearily at the effort, and headed inside the station.

"Well, bleeding Christ!" exclaimed a stout man in a dirty apron who was serving drinks

Judd Cole

behind the raw-plank bar. His next remarks suggested he didn't realize Hickok was driving for Overland. "It *is* Wild Bill Hickok! I heard a rumor you were in the territory. What brings you to these parts?"

"Six tired horses, a Concord coach, and a splintery ass," Bill retorted, for no women were in the barroom. "Set me up a jolt of Old Taylor, wouldja, Bottles?"

"I'd admire to, Wild Bill. Touch you for luck? The name's Harney McDowell. And this hombre just walked in is my boss, Dave Soss."

Bill shook hands with both. Harney was one of those overly jolly types who showed too many teeth when he smiled. In contrast, Soss, the station agent, was a serious, sickly man in his fifties with skin like yellowed ivory.

"I knew you were coming, Bill," Soss confided. "Leland told me. But I figured you weren't eager to have the fact paraded around."

" 'Preciate that, Dave. Hit me again, Harney. Not so much glass this time, okay?"

"Just give him the bottle," Soss told the bardog.

Bill nodded his thanks. "They setting out some grub in the dining room?"

"Nothing fancy. Just bean soup and biscuits. But there's plenty, and it's hot."

"Sounds like a feast."

Jimmy and Joshua came in through the back door. Jimmy nodded once, letting Bill know he'd taken a walk out back and all looked secure.

By now Hickok was starting to feel that pleasant floating sensation that meant the liquor was taking effect.

"I guess our princess from Chicago has finally got hungry," Jimmy reported with a grin. "She's in the dining room, working on her second bowl of soup."

"She even added salt," Josh chimed in, and all three men shared a good laugh.

"Boys, I'm beat out," Hickok told his companions. "I'm eating and then turning in. But I've got a hunch this place will mean trouble before the night's over. We best take turnabout on guard duty out in the yard. Joshua, you take first stint, since you look rested. Use my rifle. Wake up Jimmy for the dog watch. Jimmy, you roust me out for the last stint."

His companions nodded.

"Bill," Josh said as he accepted Bill's Winchester, "isn't it about time for Calamity Jane to butt in? After all, she usually does when you're in the company of a pretty girl."

Bill winced slightly at mention of Jane—a topic that made him as nervous as a Sioux naming the dead.

"Last I heard," he replied, "she's serving three months in an Amarillo jail for assaulting a law officer. Three, actually—I'm told she also put both his deputies out of commission."

Actually, Josh thought as he tucked the repeater across the crook of his left arm and began strolling out in the moonlit yard, having Jane around right now would be a comfort. That strike back on the Denver Road, and especially those explosive arrows, made him understand just how determined and ruthless this new enemy was.

He walked a slow, unpredictable pattern as Bill had taught him, circling the house, corrals, and outbuildings. The stock tender finished his last chores and retired to his shakedown in the hayloft. The last voices trailed into sleepy silence out in the male passengers' bunkhouse.

The individual lamps showing from the house also winked out one by one. Josh saw Wild Bill framed once in a window of the left front bedroom. Then the lamp was blown out, and only Hickok's cigar could be glimpsed, a glowing red dot.

Only one light, at the opposite end of the house, still glowed. Charlene's room, he guessed. It always took women longer to get ready for bed.

The autumn night chilled considerably, and Josh could glimpse his breath rising in steamy puffs in the moonlight. He shivered under his thin wool coat, especially when the mournful, ululating howl of coyotes sounded from the surrounding hills.

A horse nickered from the back of the corral, and Josh veered over that way, just making sure. Probably just a snake or a prowling raccoon—

A shadowy form suddenly lunged at him from behind a toolshed, and Josh had no time to bring Bill's '73 up to the ready. But a year spent traveling with the best survivor in America had taught Josh a few useful tricks in a pinch.

He dropped the rifle and applied a rolling hip-lock to break the man's charge. Before his attacker could overcome the sudden counteroffensive, Joshua managed to flip him over his back with a flying mare.

But he didn't know about the second attacker behind him, only waiting for an opportunity. Just as Joshua was about to scoop up the Winchester, a solid brass butt-plate smashed down hard on the base of his skull, just above the neck, and he dropped as if his legs had been deboned. The world went black even before he finished falling.

Hickok was almost across the threshold of deep sleep when a horse whinnied outside, the sound somehow wrong against the quiet backdrop of the night.

His eyes snapped open, his senses instantly alert. One hand reached for the gunbelt dangling off a bedpost even as he sat up, swinging his stockinged feet to the floor. He had gone to bed with his trousers on, expecting trouble. Now he quickly tightened the belt as he crossed to the window and knuckled the curtains aside, peering out into the blue-tinted moonlight.

All seemed quiet at this end of the yard. Too quiet—why weren't there horses milling in the corral? Then, from the end of the corral he couldn't see, came the frightened whicker of a horse that had smelled death blood.

He cursed as he raced out of his room and down the long hallway, charging into the bedroom at that far end without bothering to knock.

He heard a frightened scream from the bed.

"Get down on the floor!" he barked even as he threw open the window. "And *don't* light the lamp!"

Bill spotted a form moving quickly away from the corral. But he held his fire, uncertain who it was and unwilling to endanger Joshua.

"Josh!" he called out. "Sound off, lad, so I know who to shoot!"

He heard nothing from Josh, but the fleeing figure immediately opened fire on the window with a repeating rifle. The glass shattered, showering Bill in slivers and shards, and chunks of the sash blew into the room as lead hammered his position. A second rifleman had opened up, too, and Wild Bill cursed as he sprawled flat in the broken window glass, unable to get off even a shot.

The volley seemed endless, the intruders taking no chances at letting Hickok get off a shot. Only when Charlene screamed again did Bill realize she hadn't followed his order—she still lay in bed. That left her dangerously exposed.

"Damnit!" He low-crawled over, cutting his forearms and elbows, until he could grab one of her slim ankles. One quick, hard tug brought her onto the floor only moments before several slugs punched into the feather mattress, sounding like polite coughs, and puffing little white feathers all over the room.

The defensive barrage ceased, and moments later a fast drumbeat of shod hoofs told him the attackers were escaping.

Still cursing, Wild Bill groped around a little

nightstand beside the bed until he felt a few loose lucifers. He thumb-scratched one and lifted the glass chimney of the lamp, lighting the wick and turning it up.

Bill's hands, arms, and bare chest were bloody with numerous glass slices, none of them too serious but stinging like the proverbial death of a thousand cuts. Despite the fear still thudding in his temples, his first glimpse of Charlene made him forget his next breath.

She lay among the bedcovers on the floor, a stricken look on her pretty face. She wore only a chemise of thin muslin—so thin he could trace the dark, swollen protuberances of her nipples. The chemise had ridden high up on her legs, so scandalously high that Bill glimpsed a golden triangle of silky hair before she tugged the chemise lower, managing to sit up.

"You!" she got out with difficulty, still so frightened that he could see her pulse in her creamy white throat. "This . . . this is an outrage!"

Bill heard Jimmy out in the yard, calling Josh's name. In spite of his own urgency to get outside, Wild Bill was momentarily bolted in place by the erotic vignette before him.

"Don't get your bowels in an uproar," he roweled her. "You're safe from my 'unbridled lust.' "

Bill got that choice phrase from *Wild Bill, Indian Slayer*—one of the more popular dime novels that told the "true story" of James Butler Hickok.

"I surely don't *feel* safe," she assured him, boldly matching his stare although her tone re-

vealed hurt dignity. But besides pulling the chemise down a few modest inches, she made no
further attempt to cover herself.

He folded his arms over his chest, watching
her with a sly frankness. Then he laughed out-
right.

"So much for the boarding-school priss. If
you were really outraged, you'd have covered up
by now. But the truth is, you're proud of what
you got, and you *like* me looking at you."

Anger firmed her features, but Wild Bill was
gone the very next heartbeat, racing out front
of the house.

"Jimmy!" he sang out even before he spotted
his friend. "All secured?"

"Best I can tell."

"What about the kid?"

"Over here, Bill, behind the toolshed. Somebody conked his cabeza a good one, but I think
he'll be all right."

Joshua did revive quickly enough, although
he complained it felt like he'd been kicked by a
mule. However, the true extent of the damage
was discovered when they turned to the corral.

"Well, God kiss me," Hickok said quietly,
even his jaded eyes shocked by the carnage.

A total of twelve horses had all been quietly
and efficiently throat-slashed. Even as the
dazed men walked among the dead and dying
animals, one began emitting a fluttering trumpet sound as air rushed out if its collapsing
lungs.

"This is their answer," Bill announced, "to my
killing of those horses earlier."

"They missed our saddle band, at least," Jimmy pointed out. "They didn't see them up in the paddock. And they missed a few others, too. Guess you spotted them in the nick of time to save those."

"You've missed the mark," Bill corrected him in a grim voice. "Notice how many, and just *which*, horses they left, Jimmy."

Jimmy looked closer, then softly swore a mild oath. "Jerusalem! It's the six team horses."

Wild Bill nodded. "They deliberately left the tired animals. They knew one night's rest wouldn't be enough. That means they plan to attack us again, boys, between here and the next station."

Chapter Nine

Gil Brennan, Sandy Urbanski, and Rick Collins met in a deserted soddy just three miles off the Denver freight road, surrounded by the rolling grazeland of eastern Wyoming. It was a damp, chilly morning under an overcast sky the color of bog water. Brennan's mood seemed to match the weather.

"I'm *not* being 'womanish' about it," he told Urbanski coldly. "I don't see what you're acting so cocksure about, is all. Race is dead, and you two have had your horses shot out from under you. You made your brag, just a few days ago, how Hickok would be worm fodder by now and that gold in our hands. Remember?"

Urbanski's dead, obsidian stare unnerved Brennan, and despite his anger he glanced away first.

"Race ain't no loss," Urbanski countered sarcastically. "Man was a useless drunkard—it leaves more swag for the rest of us. As for them two horses, we evened *that* score last night, and then some."

Brennan's voice yielded to his anger. "The horses aren't the point, Sandy, can't you grasp that? It's *control*. I told you we want to make Hickok *think* he's in control—that way we can catch him off his guard. But so far he really is in control."

"Yeah, well, 'so far' won't mean squat once we plug Hickok," Urbanski insisted belligerently. "You best pull that pinecone outta your ass, Brennan. Out here your 'authority' ain't worth a rusted trace chain."

Brennan's tight-lipped smile seemed to cost him an effort. But he suddenly realized the danger he was in here. These two men were both killers wearing the tie-down holsters of their profession and either man would gladly shoot him for his diamond belt buckle.

"All right," Brennan conceded. "Hell, you boys are right. Hickok's clover is deep, but on this line his luck is bound to play out."

"Damn straight," Urbanski replied. "He can strut and bluff and bluster all he wants. But Bill Hickok is a done-for case."

"Don't keep selling him short like that," Brennan warned, keeping his tone more reasonable. "I think you boys are being fooled by Hickok's dandy appearance. He may wear perfume, but that man is rawhide tough."

"Tough, my sweet aunt," Rick Collins spoke

up from the doorway, where he was keeping watch for any unwanted company. "He's just sneaky, that's all, see? One of them cowards who learns how to sneak so's they avoid a fight."

Brennan knew better but refused to push these two anymore—the derringer in his breast pocket was utterly useless against them, and he knew it. They were edgy and primed for action, especially Urbanski.

"Hickok's sneaky, all right," he conceded. "They say he learned his tactics from studying Stonewall Jackson: Always mislead, surprise, and confuse your enemy. But we're going to turn his own tactics against him at Silver Wolf Pass. You boys remember what to do?"

Urbanski scowled even though he nodded. "We start to attack, then run like hell after they start some resistance. *Sneaky*," he added sarcastically.

Brennan ignored the sarcasm. "That's the gait. Both the soldiers are going to make it look like they're fighting wildcats. You fade, then ride ahead to the rendezvous point at Miller's Creek. No way in hell will Hickok and his crew be ready for a second strike only ten minutes down the road."

"*Now* who's sounding 'cocksure'?" Urbanski demanded. He took off his old campaign hat and showed Brennan a bullet hole near the crown. "That buffalo soldier siding him is a helluva shot—he damn near tagged my brainpan at six hundred yards. From a moving coach."

Brennan smiled like a magician with plenty more in his topper.

"I told you Hickok would select a crackerjack shootist for the box seat," he told Urbanski. "That's why we're going to institute another plan before we pull the false heist at Silver Wolf Pass."

"What plan? First *I've* heard of it."

"That's because it didn't occur to me until last night when I was studying this," Brennan explained, pulling an accordion-folded map from his pocket. "It's a topography map made by the Army Corps of Engineers. I won it in a poker game out in Sioux Falls."

Brennan nodded in the direction of the buckboard parked in the weed-choked yard out front. "Ricky! Pull back that canvas tarp so we can glom the load."

Collins stepped outside, shunting his Sharps to his left hand and tugging back the tarp with his right.

Out loud he sounded out the warning painted in big green letters on the sides of three wooden crates: "Dan-ger high ex-plo-sives."

"This map reminded me of a place I used to pass twice a week when I was a driver," Brennan explained. "The dynamite's been stored at my ranch since you boys boosted it from those miners near Pierre. If my plan works, it could all be over in about twenty seconds. We might have to do some digging, is all. I've got a steam-shovel crew standing by in Spearfish."

"Hell, I take your drift," Urbanski said, suddenly catching on. "Devil's Slope. That's how's come you wanted them stuck with tired horses."

Brennan nodded. "Can you picture it after one hundred pounds of dynamite has blown that rock dike away? And them below with exhausted horses in the harness?"

Collins liked it so much, he started laughing as if at a capital joke. And even the hard-bitten, cynical Urbanski gave a grudging nod of admiration.

"They'll be like ducks on a fence," he conceded. "Sometimes being sneaky is damned entertaining. But we best get humping if we want to get the charge planted. Way I kallate it, we only got maybe two hours."

Josh had a stiff, sore neck the next morning, and he could barely rotate his head. But the Denver-bound bullion coach rolled out just after daybreak, Wild Bill nursing a tired but still-plucky team. Plastered linen covered shallow yet painful glass cuts on his hands and forearms.

"The condition of these animals won't matter a jackstraw either way," he told his topside companions while they watched their three passengers board. "They rested one night on double grain rations, so they'll hold up the forty-two miles to the next station, long's they ain't pushed too hard."

He paused and nodded to Saville and Appling. "Morning, Reverend, Mr. Lawton," he greeted them, still keeping up the ruse as they filed outside, Appling picking his teeth with a spent match.

They nodded, Rabbit-Face still unable to meet Bill's frank gaze.

"And if we're attacked," Bill resumed quietly, "those horses won't be running anyway. You two remember—the very moment an attack starts, *we* take the offensive. They'll be expecting us to wage a running battle. Instead, go at 'em head-on like badgers."

"And meantime watch the soldiers," Josh put in quietly.

" 'At's right. All of us, but you especially, kid. You're sorta our personal bodyguard."

Josh nodded. "Still just a hunch, Bill?"

"It's Appling," Bill admitted quietly. "Saville is slick. But his pard has got a guilty mind."

Wild Bill touched his hat as Charlene Durant came out last, her eyes shyly slanted away from Hickok's gaze. Her hair was neatly coiffed, and she wore a blue knitted shawl against the bite of the morning air. As dust protection, she wrapped her head in a fancy scarf of poppy-colored silk sewn with sequins.

She looks good covered or uncovered, Bill realized. He took her left arm to help her up the folding step.

"Miss Durant," he said quietly, detaining her a moment. "I have every reason to think we'll be attacked again. You're *sure* you won't lay over here, take the next coach?"

"Attacked again?" she repeated in a fading voice.

"I b'lieve so, yes."

But she shook her head in determination. "I must get to Denver, Mr. Hickok. I trust you."

93

"Headstrong girl," Wild Bill remarked when he'd climbed up onto the box.

Jimmy took out the makings and built a smoke. He looked up at Josh and winked. "Ask me," he said, licking the paper, "she's determined, all right. Determined to stay real near Wild Bill Hickok."

Bill kicked off the brake and clucked at the team. "Well, nobody did ask you, old son. Keep your thoughts on the *natural* terrain."

But Jimmy wasn't quite finished roweling his friend. "Yeah, boy, a gal puts on fancy feathers like that, hell, she's dressing for a cotillion ball, not a dirty old stagecoach ride. She's preening for you, Mister Billy,"

Hickok snorted, cracking the whip over the glossy rumps of the team. "You can just forget her motivations, Jimmy. You'll bite your own teeth before you'll ever figure out a woman. He-yah, he-*yah!*"

"She's as cold as last night's pudding," Joshua scoffed.

Bill gave that remark a mysterious little grin. "What went cold last night can be heated up today. But both of you better quit dogging it and watch for trouble."

The first ten miles went by quietly enough, the landscape folded into low, stark ridges by ancient glaciers that left heaps of moraine but little screening timber. At one point they left the trail to pass a long immigrant train.

"They'll take the north fork at Silver Wolf Pass," Bill explained. "We'll take the south. Eyes to all sides, boys! They could hit us at any time now."

Joshua saw Wild Bill loosen his ivory-grip Colt .44-40s in their holsters. That gesture, like the calm, expectant look on Hickok's face, said it clearly: *The readiness is all.* Wild Bill learned that lesson early in life as a young deputy in the Kansas Territory, and he lived by that law with everything he did.

The terrain changed dramatically and quickly, showing the geologic ravages of some distant upheaval: buttes arose, scree piled at their bases, and the trail began to corkscrew around natural rock turrets. Soon cliff shadows engulfed the trail, and all three men watched in all directions.

Though gradually failing him, Wild Bill's eyes were still good enough to sweep the terrain and pick out a spot, above and to their right, where a natural rock dike held back an entire steep slope of loose talus and scree. Thousands of tons of it.

Wild Bill had once protected railroad surveying crews, and he knew exactly how their surveyors marked spots like that on their maps: *unstable landslide slope—demolish.*

"Yeah, I see it, too," Jimmy said, reading Bill's frown. "You still think tired horses won't matter today?"

Bill glanced at the trail ahead. Although it was straight again, it was now a long incline. Boulders and slag heaps blocked any escape left or right. Once again his "take the offensive" strategy seemed a pale consolation.

"Well, odds are it won't matter," Wild Bill announced, trying to convince himself.

The stagecoach climbed on, crawling across the base of the slope like a slow bug. Too late, Bill thought about hitching the saddle band onto the traces. But it would take more time now, exposed to danger, than they'd save.

When Joshua heard the first stuttering rumble he looked straight overhead, expecting another cloudburst.

But that first slow gathering of noise quickly escalated to a resounding explosion. Josh saw a huge dust cloud rise up fast like vented steam, blocking out the entire horizon. Then, in an eye-blink, it was as if the slope above them were a giant animal shaking itself off.

That impression, in turn, passed in a heartbeat, and the frightened youth saw the entire mass of rocks suddenly bearing down on them, gathering size and speed like an avalanche of gray snow. Then Charlene Durant's piercing scream from inside the coach cut into his heart like a blade, and Joshua heard the words clearly inside his skull, death-goaded from memory: *Tell me how you die, and I'll tell you what you're worth.*

Chapter Ten

Luckily for the others, however, Wild Bill Hickok did not bother, as Josh did, with philosophical thoughts at moments when death reared its head. He knew instinctively that passivity usually meant death, and that even the wrong action was almost always preferable to no action.

"Cover down!" he roared at his two friends as that swirling, choking vanguard of aroused dust engulfed them, thick as London fog.

A freight-train roar filled his ears as Wild Bill, choking and nearly blinded, leaped off the box onto the back of a wheel horse. He managed to keep his feet, reach the lead team, and straddle both horses, hanging on to fistfuls of their mane.

Their natural tendency was to try running

left, not straight, to avoid the approaching maelstrom of death. But Wild Bill knew they'd all wipe out on the scattered boulders, trapping them right in the path of the crumbling talus slope. With sheer, brute strength, Hickok used his arms as powerful reins, muscling the frightened animals back onto the main trail and holding them.

Yet—all was lost if they couldn't pull faster. Hanging on precariously, Hickok dipped his head down and gave both horses a painful bite on their sensitive ears.

"Hee-*yah*, you four-legged hellstallions, hee-*YAH*!"

Those harsh bites altered their fear to rage, and the lead pair surged forward, Wild Bill egging them mercilessly on. The dust now made the air unbreathable, choking eyes, nose, throat, and Wild Bill heard Charlene scream again when one of the first rocks reached them, a natural cannon ball as it blew a hole in one of the japanned side panels, rocking the stagecoach wildly and almost tripping up the team.

But Hickok stuck like a stubborn tick, gravel dust pelting him like buckshot, unable to see or breathe, unable even to spur the horses on with voice commands, just hanging on and uttering urgent grunting sounds like a foraging bear. Joshua, curled into the smallest ball possible atop the coach, loosed a shout of terror when a wildly hurling rock whiffed just inches past his head and crashed into the top seat, cracking it in half.

There was one horrifying moment where

teamster Hickok believed he had failed to save his passengers or himself: A second rock, a third smashed the coach and sent it careening; the bulk of the talus weight was literally pressing them like worms about to die under a boot heel.

Then—a lunging, rushing, praying *break* in the dust cloud, the roaring train commotion still ferocious and loud, but behind them, and for perhaps thirty seconds as the team slowly settled down, Wild Bill had trouble understanding they had cleared the landslide.

The conveyance lurched to a halt, and a cheer erupted behind him as he staggered around to take the roll. Jimmy and Josh, both black as coal from the dust, waved triumphantly at their bigger-than-legend driver.

"All safe inside!" John Saville reported, hanging out one window. "Though Miss Durant could use some smelling salts. Coach is damaged, Bill, but the wheels and axles appear intact."

"God's trousers!" Appling shouted, hanging out the other window. "There's no trail behind us now! Just a rock-plugged pass."

Bill called a brief rest stop so the horses could blow and the humans dust themselves off and inspect the coach closer. But even with Josh and Jimmy still excited and praising him, Bill sent them a quelling stare.

"Stonewall Jackson" was all he had to say to Jimmy. The war veteran understood immediately: as too many Union soldiers learned, sometimes you celebrate a "victory" that, in reality, is only a calculated part of your defeat.

Joshua, too, settled down and kept a close eye on the soldiers as they dusted themselves off. However, when they removed their weapons to clean them, Wild Bill and Jimmy kept their own weapons to hand.

Bill's always careful, Josh told himself. But he's got no evidence the soldiers are Brennan's guns. By now he ought to be convinced they're playing it straight. I am.

Charlene Durant, however, surprised everyone with the joyful good humor of her mood as she realized what she had just survived—and just *who* had gotten them through it.

"They warned me back in Chicago," she said with a charming smile, hopelessly dusting off her once-white shirtwaist, " 'wear black out west,' they all told me. 'It won't show the filth.' And I thought they were just lazy!"

Her eyes never left Bill while she said all this.

"Preening," Jimmy repeated in a mutter only Bill and Josh could hear.

"Maybe," Bill muttered back. "But some birds mate for life and some don't. I think she's the kind that does. Now, if you two girls are done gossiping, all right if we move this coach to Denver? I got a bonus to collect."

The damaged but still-functioning coach covered almost ten miles in the next two hours, the fresher horses in the rear now switched to the lead traces. Even with stronger leaders, the team was unwilling to move much faster than a walking man. Wild Bill didn't push them much, either, except on the occasional inclines.

He was more interested in reconnoiter. He questioned Jimmy and Joshua constantly, keeping them honest.

"Kid? What's got that eagle circling?" he called out, pointing out across a grassy swale to a line of bare hills on the horizon.

"What eag—oh, yeah, I see it." Josh squinted in the afternoon sunlight. He was precariously balanced on the half of the seat that was still bolted to solid wood. The other half, crumbled useless, the metal frame bent out like a wind-twisted shingle, was now his footrest.

"I think it's following a bobcat," Josh said suddenly. "Sure. The bobcat's on a food scent, so the eagle means to steal the meal after the cat chases it out into the open."

Bill nodded. "Good. Bobcat hates the man smell. It wouldn't hunt if there were any near it."

And he "borrowed" Jimmy's eyes the same way. "James—what's those dust puffs due west?"

"A small herd of antelope, Bill. Crossing some low sand hills. Could be—No, they're moving too fast—they've been spooked."

Bill nodded and asked Joshua to dig the field glasses out of his bedroll. The reporter took them from their case and handed them to him. Wild Bill spent at least a full minute studying the terrain to their west.

"Sure. I can't spot any men because they've moved up on us behind that long hogback ridge. Takes them fifty yards away from the road just up ahead. That's why the antelope are running

101

at right angles to the ridge—they've caught the man scent."

"Could be any men," Josh felt compelled to say.

"Kid," Bill said with his usual calm politeness, "you done good with the bobcat. You couldn't read sign like that when you first got out here. You've been a quick study. But you're not quite ready for your ranger's cap. It's not all there to read sometimes. Sometimes you have to believe it when your blood tickles you."

Bill looked at Jimmy, then Joshua. He nodded to the right, due west. "I say we've got an attack coming from behind that hogback, should hit us in about fifteen minutes."

"Suffering Moses," Jimmy swore, more impressed by Bill's confidence than the threat itself. "He done this hoodoo business during the war, too, Joshua. He was never wrong."

Josh, finally impressed into silence, quickly slid out his flipback pad and a stub of pencil, making some notes. Bill went on:

"Jimmy, I'm thinking of sustained fire with strict target discipline. Like the 107th did when you broke Sherman's picket line at Petersburg. So once targets are confirmed, you'll empty first your long gun, then your short. I'll take over immediately after your last shot while you cover and reload. We keep that pattern up—sustained fire."

Bill nodded at Joshua. "The Philly Kid here won't actually empty his short gun unless they attack at close quarters. He'll hoard his bullets while he also monitors our other guests."

Nobody topside had to ask who the guests were.

"Kid," Bill added, keeping his voice down, "I want you to have your shooter at the ready once those two Army pistoleros roll out, got it?"

"Yeah, but—"

"Stick them butts in your pocket, Joshua, and listen to me. This ain't an editorial discussion in New York. You're getting orders for combat, is that clear?"

The reporter's jaw shaped up strong. "Yessir!"

"They turn them guns in the wrong direction, you shoot to kill right now, mister. Before they can find a bead. If there's a mistake, let's err in our own favor—you catch my drift?"

Josh nodded. "Shoot first. Ask questions later." He paused a moment, then added: "If at all."

Wild Bill grinned, cracking his whip when the team began bogging down. "There's our boy! Besides that, spot their targets and see where their bullets hit. Low, wide, wild—I'm gonna predict they won't score a kill."

"See if they even adjust for battle sights," Jimmy tossed in. "Random misses mean they're just doing it purposeful-like. Just slacking it."

Jimmy looked up. "Hogback's about a half mile ahead," he reported. He pulled the watch from his fob pocket and thumbed back the cover. "Been about seven, eight minutes since your prediction."

Bill shucked out his right-hand gun and slid it through his belt, closer to hand. He already had his Winchester across his thighs. Jimmy set his with the butt plate resting on his thigh, his hand on the lever.

"Business is good for headhunters," Jimmy called out cheerfully. But Hickok's scowl reminded him just *whose* head was most valuable around here. That just made Jimmy grin wider, until Hickok, too, was forced to laugh.

"If I lose a target to distance," he told Jimmy, "I'll flip my weapon to you, if you're reloading, and you'll flip me your empty."

Jimmy nodded. He had such faith in Wild Bill's combination of sign-reading and hunch that he now slid down off the seat, kneeling on his right leg, his left braced out behind—snapping in for his favorite position, the kneeling offhand.

"It's been twelve minutes now," Josh said, and the very moment he fell silent a rifle cracked, and Jimmy rolled to his left, grunting hard on a sharp intake of breath, when a slug punched into his right thigh. The noise of impact, like a spade cutting into earth, made Josh wince.

Bill reined in, cussing, as more shots rang out from positions along the hogback ridge.

"Stick to the plan!" Jimmy got out somehow as he pushed himself up into firing position again. "I got my target!"

Jimmy's Winchester began cracking and bucking. Josh had too many things to do at once. Below, the stagecoach doors were thrown open and the sharpshooters rolled out, taking up positions. Joshua remembered, just in time, to get his own revolver out of its holster.

But too damn much was going on! Bullets thwacked into the coach, and Joshua glimpsed several men showing themselves momentarily behind the ridge, just popping up and snap-shooting with rifles.

Joshua had been in a few scrapes by now, and this one wasn't amounting to much. Jimmy's very first shots, even though poorly aimed because Jimmy was slipping into shock, very quickly broke the attack. Even before Wild Bill had to fire a shot. He did get one off, wounding a man—Joshua heard the yelp of pain, the cursing.

However, he could only catch all of this in fractional glimpses, for Josh also had to monitor the soldiers. At first he was impressed by their bold agility as they covered down behind a knoll and opened fire.

Then he quickly became aware—no bullets were thumping into the dirt close around them. Of course, that could mean the obvious, that Wild Bill and Jimmy, both using rifles, posed the serious threats, not a preacher and a drummer with short irons.

But near as Josh could tell in all the confusion, those sharpshooters were not only missing targets by yards, but making no orderly effort to adjust. Just like Jimmy predicted—random shots.

At one point the one posing as the toupee salesman cast a furtive glance up at the box. Catching Joshua's eyes, he turned away immediately and resumed his forward fire.

Now, knowing he was being observed, he

aimed better. Or so it seemed to Joshua.

Hoofbeats retreated behind the ridge, and Wild Bill called out to cease fire.

"Jesus *God* that hurts," Jimmy swore, laying his warm rifle aside to inspect his wound. "Jerusalem! It's a high pucker, Bill. At least a three-hundred-grain bullet, I'm thinking. It's got in deep, devil take it."

With Joshua and the soldiers below covering against a false retreat, Wild Bill ripped Jimmy's trousers away to inspect the wound.

"No blood spurts—that's good. Missed any major arteries."

Wild Bill had brought along a pouch filled with cornstarch to stem bleeding. He packed some into Jimmy's wound.

"That'll stop most of the bleeding until we get to Beecher's Station. Then we'll clean it out with carbolic, dig out that slug, cauterize the wound. Here, finish this off, Jimmy, for the pain."

Wild Bill pulled out the rest of the Old Taylor, the bottle Dave Soss gave him at the last station, and handed it to the wounded guard.

"Let's go, boys!" Wild Bill called out to the soldiers. "I plan to make schedule."

"I think maybe you're right to be leery of those two," Joshua reported as soon as the coach was under way.

Bill looked at him, one blond eyebrow cocked. "Sloppy patterns?"

Josh nodded. "They seemed to get neater once they caught me looking."

Bill mulled that. The news obviously didn't sit too well with him. He slanted a worried glance at Jimmy, whose face was twisted against the excruciating pain in his leg.

"Kid, take Jimmy's rifle and reload it. Take his bandolier, too, and put it on. It's going to be me and you from here to Beecher's Station."

"Think they'll hit us again that quick?"

Wild Bill's eyes raked the terrain before he answered. "I think they'll hit us again, yes, and I think they'll hit soon. Real soon. There was no heart to that assault just now, even though they got lucky and tagged Jimmy. I think it was more like Stonewall Jackson's kind of fighting. This Gil Brennan likes to play at 'tactics.' "

Bill cracked the blacksnake, and the horses wearily began to pick it up to a trot. He looked at Josh again. "Get set, Longfellow. This next time won't be so easy. They'll come right down our throats, and we'll also have our hands full with those two below."

By now Jimmy had quaffed the liquor and was floating on a sea of alcohol and pain delirium. His eyes met Joshua's.

"Movement to contact!" Jimmy barked out. "Recruits, you will *not* fire your goddamned ramrods into the goddamned pine trees!"

Wild Bill howled with mirth, sharing some distant, ghastly memory with his old battle companion. But Joshua only stared out into the fading sunlight, feeling the weight of the cross-chest bandolier, praying to God to make him brave, feeling Jimmy's delirious words slide down his back like ice.

Chapter Eleven

"Dobber!" Sandy Urbanski called out. "The hell you boys doin' out here in the open? You three're s'pose to wait behind the cottonwoods 'til I give the high sign."

Sandy's blood bay gelding splashed quickly and easily across the gravel ford at Miller's Creek. Rick Collins, massive in the saddle, followed on his big claybank, eyes watching the three men who sat their saddles on the south bank. Flanking Dobber Ulrick were AJ Clayburn and Waco McKinney—all three fired by Leland Langford when Overland cleaned house in the Dakota Division.

"AJ here was just saying some things, is all," Dobber replied in his hill-country twang.

Sandy took out the makings and shaped a smoke while he spoke. The ridged scar tissue under his eye matched the ugly slash formed by his scowling mouth.

"Things?" he repeated. "More a them stories AJ learnt from them bog-trotters back in Loo'zana?"

AJ held his face in a deadpan, refusing to argue with a know-it-all like Urbanski. But the washed-out cowboy, Waco McKinney, had a reckless mouth and liked to scrap.

"Laugh it up, big man," he told Sandy. "We was all there watching it happen. That slope shoulda crushed the coach like a dung beetle. But Hickok pulled it clear somehow."

"This ain't the first time, neither," Dobber pitched in. "Look how the ambush with your fancy explodin' arrows didn't touch him. Now, Devil's Slope . . . and I'm not countin' three or four dozen *more* times he's escaped death in his lifetime."

Urbanski looked at Rick, and *damned* if he didn't look skittish, too. Urbanski swore out loud, his cigarette hanging on to his lower lip.

"Nerve up, you damned squaws! It was what he done to Race, wunnit? Stringin' him up on display? It's got alla yous scairt spitless."

Dobber's dull features suddenly looked dangerous. Sandy reminded himself about the slim throwing knife tucked into Dobber's right boot.

"It ain't just Injins that talk up Hickok's charmed life," Waco pointed out. "Nor just squaws that believe it."

Sandy shook his head like they were all pathetic and pitiable. "Never mind all them stories your maw-maws told about Rawhead and

Bloody Bones. Hickok is just meat and bones like the rest of us."

"Then how's come he don't *die* like the rest of us?" Waco flung at him. "That bastard's got big medicine from somewheres."

Sensing a revolt on his hands, and with time passing quickly, Urbanski switched tactics. After all, *he* wanted to claim that reward for killing Hickok. These superstitious chawbacons were playing right into his hands.

"All right," he told them, his tone less caustic. "You three just settle your hocks behind the trees and watch me and Ricky. We're leaving our horses on pickets way out of sight from here. Then we're taking up prone positions in them hawthorn thickets yonder, and we *will* send Hickok to the big reservation. If we kill him, will you boys kill the team? We won't have a good angle from the thickets."

All three men nodded.

"Kill Hickok," Waco said, "and with the darky already wounded, hell, maybe Saville and Appling will earn their cut by killing the rest."

"I don't care how it plays out," Sandy insisted. "Just so that coach gets stopped here. And just so there's enough of us to help Ricky lift that strongbox after we blow it loose and haul it out. Brennan claims he's got a safecracker lined up who knows Wells Fargo locks."

Sandy spurred his horse, but then reined in again to turn and shout behind the trio of men: "We miss it this time, boys, we're liable to miss the roundup and payoff. Don't forget how open the country gets after Beecher's Station."

"You just bragged how you're going to free Hickok's soul," Waco called back. "You do that much, we'll handle the rest."

Following Wild Bill's instructions, Joshua used a rolled-up neckerchief for a bandage, knotting it snugly around Jimmy's wounded thigh. The cornstarch did a good job of clotting the blood, and so far Jimmy had suffered no great blood loss.

"But he's shock-simple," Wild Bill explained to Josh. "Don't forget the human body's mostly water. A three-hundred-grain bullet has got enough velocity, it sends a shock wave through all that water. I've felt it before myself. It's like a dozen mules kicking inside you all at once. Jolts your brain, too."

"God dawg, boys!" Jimmy abruptly roared out. "Worm castles and embalmed beef!"

Despite the trouble they all faced, Wild Bill chuckled at the words. "He means hardtack and canned meat. He's back in the war now. Bullets didn't kill you, the grub would."

But Josh could see that Wild Bill, who was not one to reminisce, had been mulling something closely for the past mile or so. Suddenly he stared at Joshua. "Why, pitch it to hell!"

"Pitch what to hell, Bill?"

"This—what I'm doing. I'm *damned* if I'll haul my own executioners another foot. We got enough to fret about, Longfellow. We're checking two items off the worry list right now. Fair and square, every man gets his chance. Stay up here and cover me, kid. Haw! *Haw!*"

Wild Bill reined in the team, set the brake, and wrapped the reins around it. Then he quickly leaped down to the ground. He stepped back about ten feet from the coach. "Sergeant Saville! Corporal Appling! Front and center!"

Hickok had pushed his canvas duster back, exposing both Peacemakers. His eyes narrowed to slits, and he watched both soldiers as they climbed out of the coach, their faces curious.

Jimmy, drunk and pain-delirious, shouted out, "No quinine for the coloreds, boys! Nor the Irish! Give 'em purgatives!"

"Hush, Sergeant Davis," Bill called up, and Jimmy did quiet down some.

"What seems to be the problem, Brother Hickok?" Saville asked, using his preacher tone.

"Hell with that," Hickok snapped. Charlene stared out the window, not understanding any of this.

"I know you're Gil Brennan's gun-throwers, bought and paid for," Hickok told them. He watched them both close, especially their hands. In an eyeblink Hickok had drawn both Colts, covering the two.

"Bill, you are mighty mistaken," Saville retorted. "We've both got copies of our orders from General Durant in our—"

"General Durant?" Charlene cut in. "How do you know my fath—"

"Shut up," Hickok snapped at her.

"Bill," Saville protested, "this is—"

"Stow it," Hickok ordered him tersely. "I know by now when men are watching for a shot at my back. Now you're getting a fair chance to kill me. Better than fair, because there's two of you. Now pull out your shooters, nice and easy, and tuck them into your belts."

"Bill, you're—"

"Shh! I got *no* slack left in these triggers, Sarge. Don't make me so much as twitch. Ease them guns out . . . that's it, slow and easy. Now muzzles behind your belts . . . that's the gait."

"Mr. Hickok!" Charlene Durant protested. "I demand to know what is going on."

But Wild Bill had his hands full monitoring the sharpshooters.

"Josh," he said, "come down here and talk to Miss Durant before I shoot her."

She protested again and tried to push open the door on Bill's side. But his left leg shot out hard, kicking it shut in her face. "Sit tight," he ordered her.

"I will *not!* You are obviously goading my father's troops into a showdown! This is . . . Why, it's murder!"

Joshua climbed in on the far side, said something low and urgent in her ear, and Charlene fell silent, though she turned her head.

"All right," Bill said when both men had their weapons secured behind their belts, butts protruding. "Hands straight out from your sides, that's it. Higher, lift 'em higher, straight out to the sides just like louse inspection. *There* you go."

Eyes never leaving the men, Wild Bill tucked his own guns into his waistband. He brought his arms straight up like theirs.

113

"Two against one," he announced. "Make your move, boys."

"And if we don't?" Appling demanded.

"Then I'll go first."

Charlene, eyes closed tight, emitted a little moan of fear and revulsion. But Joshua knew exactly what Hickok was doing, and he approved. Bill's chief responsibility was to get this coach to Denver, and with Jimmy useless to him right now, these suspected traitors had to be shot.

"Bill," Appling pleaded, "Brennan *thinks* we're on his payroll, but—"

"Shut your damn mouth," Saville cut him off, and now Joshua lost his last vestige of doubt about Hickok's instincts. These men, too, were Gil Brennan's minions.

"I saw it right off in your eyes, Appling," Bill said. "Saville is good, but you're poor shakes as a liar. Make your play, one of you, or I'll slaughter you where you—"

Saville's hand moved to his gun, Appling's a heartbeat behind. Wild Bill beat both men. But by the time he'd plugged Saville, Appling had ducked wildly to one side, getting off a shot.

Wild Bill felt a sharp tug as the slug passed through the left armpit of his duster. But he quickly pivoted on his right heel, following Appling and drilling him in the forehead before he got off another shot.

The "preacher's" eyes were still open, the death rattle noisy in his throat.

"Dust thou art," Wild Bill recited quietly, "and unto dust shalt thou return."

He tossed a quick finishing shot into Saville. "Joshua?" he called out quietly.

The reporter's mouth had gone dry, and he had to pry his tongue from the roof of his mouth. "Yeah?"

"What kind of law were we instructed to uphold for this mission?"

"Gun law," Joshua replied.

Bill nodded. "Just a reminder. Now help me move Jimmy down into the coach. There's a seat left free for him now, so we'll stretch him out."

Jimmy, though still ranting at times, was cooperative. The two men got him down off the box and into the coach.

"Well, are you feeling better, Mr. Hickok?" Charlene demanded coldly. "Your day must feel complete now—you've killed somebody."

Bill gave her an uninterested look. "Sometimes it's kill or be killed, Miss Durant," Bill replied calmly. "Those two were hired to kill me and help steal this gold. They were both soldiers from Fort Bridger, your father's command. But evidently your old man is as gullible as you are. I've no doubt his 'handpicked' men would have raped you before they killed you."

Her face flushed with rage, but Wild Bill ignored her. Joshua saw him glancing out the open door at the two bodies, a speculative glint in his eyes.

"What?" Joshua demanded.

"That attack back at Silver Wolf Pass was a feint," Bill replied. "They could have pressed it harder, but they didn't. That means they're lay-

115

ing for us. And according to the map Leland gave me, the ideal place to attack would be the creek coming up. It's a gravel ford surrounded by trees and thickets."

Again Wild Bill's gunmetal gaze cut to the dead bodies. This time a little grin twitched at his lips.

"Now killing is funny?" Charlene fumed.

"I wish you'd shut up," Bill told her calmly. "You whine too much. Joshua?"

"Yeah?"

"Climb topside and get that coil of new rope tied to the saddle I used."

"Sure, but—what for?"

"You'll see in a minute," Wild Bill promised.

"He wants to hang the bodies on display," Charlene taunted.

Bill nodded. "In a manner of speaking. Since these two dead soldiers were intended as our military escort, that's just what they're going to be. Quick, kid, get me that rope."

Jimmy regained awareness and looked at Charlene Durant. "Lord, it's an angel, and a pretty one! Let us cross the river and rest in the shade."

"Here they come, Ricky," Sandy Urbanski gloated from his position in the hawthorn thickets overlooking the freight road below. "I hear the tug chains jingling."

Sandy jacked a round into the chamber of his Yellow Boy, careful not to bang it against anything—he still hadn't replaced the worn sear. Rick lowered the breechblock of his Big Fifty and inserted a round into the chamber.

"There," Sandy said as the lead team first emerged around a long bend. "There they . . ."

He trailed off, his jaw going slack in surprise. "What in Sam Hill? It's Saville and Appling, ain't it? Sure it is, driving the stage."

The coach, holding the same stately speed as a hearse, creaked closer to the shallow creek. Now Sandy frowned.

"Christ, they drunk? Lookit how Saville's head is flopping around. . . . Jesus! Lookit the blood on Appling's face!"

"Sandy," Collins cut in, his voice high with fright. "D-D-Danny's got a buh-bullet hole in the middle of his fuh-fuh-forehead! He's . . . gawd-*damn*, Sandy, they're both *dead!*"

"Listen to yourself," Sandy scoffed. "Dead men don't hold reins and drive stagecoaches. Damn them," he added when the sudden drumming of hoofbeats erupted behind the stand of cottonwoods. "Sonny and them other ignut bastards have took off."

Rick eased his hammer back to half cock and scrambled to his feet, remarkably quick for a man weighing almost three hundred pounds. "I'm gettin' the hell outta here, too. Them dead men are *too* driving that coach!"

Ricky bolted toward the horses.

"Rick!" Sandy shouted at his retreating partner. "Rick, damnit man, nerve up! It's just more of Hickok's parlor tricks—he . . . *Rick!* Damn your chicken guts, get back here!"

But it was hopeless. Now that he was left

Judd Cole

alone, Urbanski took one last look before he, too, bolted.

"This is sickness—*mad*ness," Charlene Durant fumed. "And now you're simply going to dump the bodies?"

She stood beside the coach, arms akimbo, watching as Wild Bill and Joshua quickly untied the carefully propped-up dead men. She had to leap aside, gasping in revulsion, when Saville's body landed beside her in an unceremonious heap. A dead hand flopped onto her foot, and she leaped back.

Wild Bill jerked a thumb upward, showing her the vultures already swooping in low circles. "Whatever they don't eat the coyotes will gnaw. I got a rule, princess: Never bury the enemy unless they smell."

He grunted hard with effort as he threw Appling off on the opposite side, dumping him like a sack of garbage. Joshua saw Wild Bill fretting at a spot of blood on his cuff. "Won't wash out," he muttered.

Hickok sat quietly for about twenty seconds, just listening.

"Keep a sharp eye out, Longfellow," he said finally. "We scared 'em off, but they might rile up once their fear passes."

Bill climbed back over to the driver's side of the box and glanced impatiently down at the pouting woman.

"Let's go, sugar britches, all aboard!"

But she stubbornly stood her ground. "After what you just did? Rigging up dead men to—"

118

"Look, sister, whatever pounds nails is a hammer. There was an ambush waiting for us here, and without Jimmy we didn't stand a snowball's chance. What I did *worked*. The point is to live on until you can win."

"Win *what?*" she demanded.

The frank look Bill gave her made her flush. "Whatever's worth winning, that's what. Now, get inside before I put you there."

Wild Bill suddenly cracked the whip, and she shrank back, fearful. But a moment later she got inside, and Hickok taunted her with his laugh as the battered coach rolled forward.

Chapter Twelve

There were some Indians, Wild Bill explained to Joshua as the stagecoach eked out the slow miles, who refused to return to a place within twenty-four hours after someone had just been killed. They believed the vengeful spirit had one day to find and possess a new body. Bill said plenty of whites believed the same thing—and maybe that was why there was no immediate attack. This was literally a death coach.

Two miles shy of Beecher's Station, Joshua spotted billowing clouds of dark smoke smudge the sunset. Soon Bill, too, could discern them.

"They've attacked the station," Hickok muttered. He whipped the nearly exhausted horses up to their best pace, perhaps six miles per hour. "Be ready for a set-to," he added. "They might be laying for us."

There was no sign of gun-throwers when they wheeled into the hoof-packed yard at Beecher's Station. But their signature had been left everywhere, from the still-smoldering ruins of the hay barn to the charred, half-destroyed station house.

Two men waited in the yard, rifles in the crook of their arms. One was in his late thirties, balding, with a big soup-strainer mustache; the other, much younger and strong as a farmer's bull—except, Josh noticed, there was a homemade crutch under his left arm.

"I'm Burl Leavitt, station manager," the oldest one greeted them. "Big fella's Yancy, a blacksmith for the Overland Line."

"Pleased," Wild Bill said curtly, adding: "Anybody killed?"

Leavitt, whose glassy eyes and slurred speech smelled alcohol-induced, shook his head.

"The two women who cook and clean slipped away and made a run for the next station."

He nodded at the limping blacksmith. "Yancy was out here working when the attack commenced. He tried to put out the barn fire. But they shot him."

"They was aiming for the dirt around my feet," Yancy explained. "Trying to make me dance. One bullet caught my heel. It ain't bad damage."

He pointed to the ruins of the barn, which still gave off a pleasant heat in the evening chill. "It was some kind of fancy fire arrow. And I seen Sandy Urbanski right after, still holding a crossbow. He had his face covered, like the others,

121

but I seen that big scar of his. He's Gil Brennan's crime boss."

Wild Bill swung down off the box and stretched his back, gazing around at the damage. He stuck a slim Mexican cigar between his teeth but didn't light it yet. Instead, he opened the door of the coach and swung down the step for Charlene, handing her down.

"He's breathing easy," she reported when Bill leaned inside to check on Jimmy.

"Got any medicines here?" Wild Bill asked Leavitt.

But the station manager was too drink-addled to focus on the question.

"Ask anybody knows me," he said, as if thinking out loud more than speaking. "I came out west on account the damned lying railroads advertised it as a grower's paradise. But dry-farming out here is a fool's game. And those with no water for irriga—"

"Your only problem," Yancy cut in impatiently, "is how you're always searching for answers in the bottom of a whiskey glass. I shoulda reported you to Leland—"

"Look, have you got medicines here?" Wild Bill cut in impatiently. "We've got a wounded man needs surgery."

"There's laudanum in the kitchen cabinet," Yancy replied for the distraught agent. "And maybe some chloroform."

Wild Bill enlisted Josh, Burl, and Yancy to help him carry Jimmy inside the damaged station. The back half of the building, though smoke-damaged, was otherwise intact. They

122

laid Jimmy on a leather-web bed usually used by drivers.

He had regained consciousness and stopped raving, though his face was drawn tight from fighting the pain.

"Hickok," he said weakly, "you're too wicked to ever be pitied. I took this bullet for you."

"Better you than me," Bill replied with the cynical bravado of battle vets. "Maybe I'll get lucky and kill you digging it out."

"Dry socks," Jimmy muttered as he went under again.

"Man's crazy," Yancy said. "His socks are dry."

"What in God's name are we going to *do?*" Burl fretted from the doorway, his voice whiny, his shoulders slumped in defeat. "The road's out at Devil's Slope. No coaches can get through 'til it's cleared. See? See it? I told Leland, I said it's a bad mistake to take on Brennan's—"

"Whack the cork," Wild Bill snapped at him. "All your bawling won't unscramble an egg. Leland wanted gun law, and that's what he got. Now we've got to stick it out until the job's done, that's all. Joshua?"

"Yeah?"

"How's that sore neck?"

"Better. What do you need?"

"Hear that, Burl?" Hickok said. "This kid's just turned twenty, city-sired, and he's up to fighting fettle. Kid, when we finish up here, take my rifle and climb up on top the house. Sing out if you see anybody. Burl?"

". . . slaughter us like rats," the agent was

muttering to himself. Wild Bill cursed, but left him alone.

"Yancy?"

"What?"

"Besides the women, has anyone been sent for help?"

"Stock tender was sent to give a report to the U.S. Marshals at Cheyenne. But that's still a far piece south from here. Best we can do. There ain't nary telegraph wire strung out this way yet, there being no government to speak of in the Dakota Territory."

Wild Bill listened, and it bothered Joshua to see that Hickok's usual face—slightly amused, unflappable—now looked tired and troubled, showing some age and wear.

"Any way you slice it," Bill told them, "Brennan's bunch still have plenty of time to make their play. Soldiers out west are stretched mighty thin, and what few there are—hell, they're mostly tied up chasing bust-outs from the reservations."

The men had all drifted back into the common room by now, its front wall half demolished by the fire. Charlene Durant, busy carrying a pail of water to heat on the iron stove, caught Bill's eye. She had already torn one of her muslin chemises into strips of clean bandage cloth.

"Say!" he exclaimed. "I just remembered— your father will be expecting you, won't he? There should be a light patrol on that Denver road once he realizes you're late."

She flushed and looked sheepish, surprising

Joshua, who didn't know she was capable of humility.

"Not really," she confessed. "I didn't tell him I was on my way. I thought it would be romantic and instructive to tour the West a little by stagecoach."

"Romantic and instructive," Hickok repeated woodenly.

"Well, yes. So many eastern dudes are doing so nowadays, it's all the rage even in the ladies' press."

"Ladies' press," Bill repeated, giving her a look that made her flush deeply.

"What?" she demanded.

He ignored her. "That explains it, then. I wondered how your old man would be that stupid and let you take a stagecoach on *this* line."

"He ordered me not to, actually. He's expecting me next month—and by train."

Bill looked at the pail. "That water for Jimmy?"

She nodded.

"Can you take the sight of blood?"

Again she nodded. "When I was just twelve I was sort of volunteered as a surgeon's orderly for the Union field hospital at Stone's River. My family's home was only a quarter mile from the battle."

Bill's tone altered somewhat. "Well, maybe you *are* Jimmy's angel. You know how to administer chloroform?"

She nodded. "There's not much to it. But it's risky."

"What ain't?" Bill retorted as he headed back

Judd Cole

into the room where they'd put Jimmy. "Bring that water in when it's heated. Joshua, climb up on top the house. Watch yourself."

Josh headed toward the burned-out front of the house, Bill's .44–40 Winchester in his left hand. Charlene Durant's voice made him pause.

"Is he always such a *hard* man, Joshua? I had the impression Wild Bill Hickok was more gallant."

A dozen different answers occurred to the young journalist. How many scrapes had he shared with Hickok in the past year or so? And yet he knew so little about the man, about what he felt and thought. In truth Bill Hickok, the toast of the American press, the living legend, was a lonely, haunted man who had whipped his fear but never quite his despair.

"Gallant?" Josh finally said. "He is, in his way. Read this. It's a rough draft for part of my next story."

He handed her his flip-back pad, opened to a neatly written page.

" 'The decisions Wild Bill makes on this perilous journey,' " she read aloud, " 'the behaviors that strike the rest of us as barbaric—history will record them and men continue to honor them. America has reached a critical crossroads in her young destiny, and now the rule of law is on the line. If these lawless road gangs triumph over the courageous teamsters, our government may be doomed for all time.

" 'Wild Bill has little formal education, but he senses that democracy's fate hangs in the balance—and his life is committed, as is Jimmy Davis's, to the cause of freedom.' "

Joshua was too tired, too scared to say all that. Besides, he was jealous. She had no eyes for any man but Hickok.

Charlene looked up, her eyes shining. "Oh, Joshua, I had no idea you could write like this. It's . . . why, it's grand, and just—just elegant!"

"Thanks," he said, pride swelling inside him at the admiration in her tone. "I guess to answer your original question, Wild Bill is as hard as he needs to be, no more."

He started to head outside again. She surprised him pleasantly by calling out behind him:

"Joshua?"

He turned around, and she flashed him a smile as big as Texas. "Be careful out there. You're a very brave young man. You remind me of all those courageous boys I treated at Stone's River."

Joshua exulted in all this attention from such a charming beauty. However, Burl Leavitt had to upset the cart. He had been standing alone in a dark corner, muttering to himself. Now he spoke up, fear tightening his voice.

"*Brave!* Huh. Fool's gold, that's what brave is. Hickok can't save us now, nor this tadpole neither. We're *all* dead as Paiute graves."

His words hung in the air like a rotten odor that everyone smelled but no one wanted to mention.

"When you get a chance," Josh told Charlene,

127

Judd Cole

"lock up all the liquor. I hope he's some use to us once he sobers up."

Wild Bill and Charlene Durant proved to be an efficient and capable surgical team.

Charlene soaked a pad in chloroform and kept Jimmy under, watching him closely—the pad had to be held up only in brief doses or the patient could quickly succumb. On the other hand, too little of it and the pain could suddenly become unbearable.

Hickok quickly used a flame-sterilized wire to locate the slug. Then he bent the wire into a hook and dug the flattened lead slug out with the help of his clasp knife. A quick carbolic-acid wash of the wound was followed by an even quicker cauterization to close the wound while it was clean.

"It'll hurt like holy hell when that chloroform wears off," Wild Bill said wearily when the surgery was finally over. "We'll make sure he gets laudanum for the pain. I wish we'd had morphine powder to pack in the wound."

"You've cut a few bullets out in your time," she praised him. "Including, I've read, one from your own leg?"

"It was only thirty-one-caliber," he scoffed. "That's like pulling out a splinter. Didn't make sense to ride fifty miles just to pay a doctor two dollars. I'm going outside to wash up and look around."

"I'll take a quick bath and then get some food cooking," she offered, continuing to show a new

128

side to her personality, one brought out by adversity.

Bill stepped quietly out through the charred remains into the nighttime chill. A newly risen three-quarter moon lighted the very tips of distant mountains like silver patina.

"All secure, kid?" he called overhead as he rinsed at a hand pump in the yard.

"Looks quiet from up here," Josh called back. "But I'm sure hungry. My ribs're scraping my spine."

"I'll bring you out some hot grub shortly. Don't skyline yourself."

Wet and shivering in the night air, Bill dried his face and hands with a bandage cloth they hadn't used. Then he began circling the house on foot in the clear moonlight.

Yancy, despite his wounded foot, had taken care of the team. Now he was standing guard near the corral, where nearly a dozen horses had escaped harm in the raid. They had chased off the attackers just in time.

"You won't find their tracks, Wild Bill," he called out. "Urbanski and them timed it so a hard rain wiped out most of their sign. I looked. They could be holed up any number of places around here. At least the rain put the fire out."

Yancy was right. Wild Bill found a few fresh tracks of shod horses. But they washed out after a few yards, obliterated by rain runoff from the low hills around them. It would require a pure-quill Indian tracker to follow it now.

Back inside, the chloroform stink still permeated their makeshift operating room, and

Jimmy was still peacefully sleeping. Wild Bill found Charlene in a front bedroom. She had hung blankets over the burned-out doorway to give herself some privacy.

"You decent?" he called from his side of the blanket.

"Yes, come in," she called back.

A lone tallow candle cast a golden light on her as she worked a horn comb through her long, tangled tresses. Bill smelled clean skin and the faint lilac odor of her soap. She had changed into a fancy serge dress—Bill could see the frilled cuffs of the embroidered undersleeves visible beneath the ermine lappets of the sleeves.

Those pretty blue forget-me-not eyes watched him from under long, sleepy lashes. The smile she gave him was restive, as if she harbored secret ideas.

"Interesting smile," he greeted her. "What's it mean?"

"Maybe it means I'm curious, Mr. Hickok."

"About what, Miss Durant?"

"Maybe," she said, setting the comb aside, "I'm one of those curious girls who wonders how close she can get to the fire without being burned?"

He watched how her unrestrained hair gleamed like polished hardwood. "That works out just right," he assured her, "because *I'm* one of those curious fellows who wonders when there's fire behind a girl's smoke."

By now only inches separated them. Wild Bill tossed his hat aside and swept her up in his arms, kissing her full on the lips. Her soft contours molded to him, and her mouth eagerly accepted his. If Bill had expected a little fight from her, he was instead surprised by the ardor of her response.

"Does that answer your question?" she teased him when they finally broke for air.

Bill, his face still hot from their kiss, picked up his hat and shook the dust from it, watching her in the flattering candlelight.

"It answers one," he told her thoughtfully. "But it raises some others."

"Such as . . . ?"

"Mr. Hickok?" Burl Leavitt's voice called from beyond the blanket. But Bill was still looking at Charlene with narrowed eyes.

"Such as," he replied, "why could I swear, when I see you in this light with your hair down, that I've seen you someplace before?"

"I'm sure I don't know. I've certainly never seen *you*. In person, I mean."

"Mr. Hickok?" Burl called again.

"Be right there," he replied in the direction of the other room. Turning to watch Charlene again, he added gallantly: "Perhaps it's just wishful thinking on my part. Your beauty is exceptional."

"I'm told you know something on that subject, and I'm quite flattered."

He bowed slightly and turned to leave. He was about to sweep the blanket aside when she called his name. Hickok turned around.

"If you wish to see more of me," she said, her voice throaty now, "I would not object."

" 'More' in which sense, Miss Durant?"

"Whichever sense you want it to mean," she retorted frankly. "Just so you come back again."

"I intend to," he promised her. "The kiss settled that."

Out in the common room, Burl had heated up a big pot of coffee and got himself half sobered up. Yancy, too, had come inside for a cup.

"Mr. Hickok," Burl said sheepishly, "I'm sorry for going puny on you. I was okay during the shooting part. But then with the fire and all—well, I wasn't careful, and I knocked back too damn much who-shot-John before Yancy cut me off. What do you want us to do?"

Charlene came out behind them and went into the kitchen.

"She's gonna set out some grub shortly," Bill told them. "Everybody eats something to keep their strength up. No more liquor. Yancy, is your forge and bellows still intact?"

The blacksmith nodded.

"Good," Bill told him. "Tomorrow, at first light, I want you to true the back left tire on the coach. It got bent a little in the rockslide."

Yancy nodded.

"Soon as we finish up here," Bill added, "you two push that coach right out into the center of the yard. I want it wide open, so anybody who wants to get at it needs to show himself in moonlight. Burl, you'll be in charge of setting up a guard. It'll be you, Joshua, Yancy. I recommend four-hour stints."

"But where're you gonna be?" Yancy asked. His eyes cut toward the blanket of Charlene's bedroom, but Hickok chose to ignore the crude hint.

"Not here," he replied. "I've had my belly full of all this swiping at the branches of our problem. So I'm going right for the roots."

"Gil Brennan?" Burl said, wiping dry lips on the back of his hand, which still trembled slightly.

Hickok nodded. "Leland marked his ranch on my map. It's only forty miles northeast from here, right?"

Burl nodded. "But it's well-fortified, Bill. You'd be riding into a mare's nest."

"I'm being well-paid to do it. You two just remember: Get that wagon positioned out in the open. And don't let down your guard. They could hit again at any moment. I'll be back sometime tomorrow."

"God go with you, Wild Bill," Yancy called behind him. "Gil Brennan's spread is like those places Mexican generals hide out at. And he's got a small army on his payroll. They capture you, Bill, it'll be slow, hard dying."

"Yancy," Bill replied from a deadpan, "quit sugarcoating it and tell me what you *really* think."

Chapter Thirteen

Gil Brennan stretched his legs, luxuriating in the feel of satin sheets smooth as a young girl's skin. This was his favorite part of the day, waking up with a willing woman beside him, eager to sate his lust without requiring love talk to justify it.

He could feel Gina's weight on the bed beside him, and it brought a smile to his face even before his eyes coaxed themselves open. But instead of the sweet honeysuckle smell of her perfume, Gil smelled . . .

His eyes snapped open suddenly as he realized someone was smoking a cigar.

"Gina, what—*Christ!*"

He had pushed up on one elbow, twisted around to his concubine, and then nearly died of fright right there in bed when he met the cold, gunmetal gaze of Wild Bill Hickok.

That first strong, heart-jolting shock of recognition was followed by a second when Brennan realized exactly where Hickok had tucked the muzzle of his Colt .44.

"Jesus, Wild Bill, please don't shoot."

Bill inclined his head in the direction of the pretty but sore-used blonde who sat, poker rigid, in a wing chair at one side of the huge master bedroom. She clutched a skimpy silk wrapper that flattered her womanly figure.

"Won't be requiring her services after you're gelded, will you, Brennan?"

Hickok sat, quite relaxed, with his back propped against the bed's carved-mahogany headboard. Early-morning sunlight turned the velvet draperies a glowing red.

"Cute little love nest," Hickok said scornfully. "I can smell the opium stink, too. No wonder you've hired jayhawking trash to steal federal gold—the drug has you off your head."

All this was too much for Brennan, who still hadn't quite comprehended that Hickok had breached his security. He remained as still as Gina. "But how . . . ?"

He trailed off, but Hickok knew what he wondered. *How did anyone penetrate to my inner sanctum?*

"Let's just say that your payroll will be a little lighter this month," Bill replied. "And by the way—most of those 'guards' of yours, Brennan, ain't worth a plugged peso."

"Few men are, Wild Bill. Both of us know that."

"Maybe," Hickok agreed. "But one difference is I don't count on inferior men. You do. That's why you're on the verge of a mutiny that will sink you."

"Who . . . who told you so?"

Hickok laughed. "Fellow name of History, I believe it was. But even if your own swine don't eat you, you've made a stupid mistake in heisting federal gold and killing soldiers. Don't you know there's prosecutors already out west, taking depositions and putting fellows like you in prison—or worse? Matter of a few months, at most, and you'll be wearing Uncle Sam's ball and chain."

Bill wagged the gun slightly, and Brennan recoiled. "Assuming," Bill added, "that I've become too civilized lately for Spanish revenge."

Despite his fear, Brennan was slowly gaining some confidence. After all, he was still alive. Hickok could have killed him by now, but he must want something. A *deal* . . . even now Brennan's scheming mind sought a way to horse-trade.

"You *are* too civilized to simply kill me, Bill. You're not a cold-blooded murderer."

"Sounds like we're good friends, huh? I mean, that you know me so well. Where was it we met? I forget now."

"Great minds think alike, Bill, you know that. Now, hanging Race's body up like you did, with the sign and all—that was just common vigilante tricks, no imagination at all. But I have to hand it to you, Bill—the 'dead men driving' trick yesterday? *That* was pure Wilkie Collins."

"Gil," the woman cut in, her tone disgusted, "you're just making it worse with all your foolish talk—"

"Shut your damn mouth," he snapped as if she were a cur who had irritated him.

"So you liked that little trick?" Bill said pleasantly.

"Don't get me wrong. An intelligent man would know right off it was a ruse. But your genius was in knowing most of those men were just ignorant enough to be scared off. It was a calculated risk, and you pulled it off. My hat's off to you."

"So you're thinking I value your praise, is that it? One superior man to another?"

"Why—no, not exactly, I don't suppose. Mainly I was just making the point that we both know men well. Read them well. It sets us—I mean, certain men apart from the majority. That's all I meant."

Hickok blew a few lazy smoke rings. "Then you tell me something, reader of men. What makes you so bedrock certain I *won't* kill you? I killed those crooked soldiers, so why not the man who actually hired them?"

"Because you want something from me. A deal. Somehow or other I'm useful to you."

Bill nodded. "All right, you're not stupid. That's partway right. I do want something."

More hope worked into Brennan's face. "A cut of the swag, right?"

Bill shook his head. "No. I want you to call off your dogs. Let this coach get through."

Brennan looked startled, then suspicious.

"This coach? But what about future gold shipments?"

"That will be somebody else's watch."

Brennan laughed, forcing it a little. "No offense, but that doesn't sound like Wild Bill Hickok."

Bill looked at Gina. "There he goes again, my good buddy."

"So you're telling me all I have to do is call back my men for this one shipment?"

Bill nodded. Brennan still couldn't figure the angle. On the face of it, he didn't like the delay in placing a bid for the Exposition Bank in San Francisco, which was now being offered for sale. It would be preferable if Hickok would just take a share of the gold.

But failing that, this odd offer at least had the merit of leaving Brennan's operation intact. Something occurred to him, and he suddenly smiled.

"Ahh, I think I understand, Bill. There is, after all, the question of your public reputation, what with you being so much in the press. A . . . private treaty between us leaves that reputation healthy as, once again, the living legend comes through."

"There you go, seeing right through me. Do we have a deal? This coach gets through?"

"Just so I understand—that's it? Just cancel this job?"

Hickok nodded. "That's it. You agree to do that, I let you go now. But I want you to understand: If you cross me, I'll hunt you down and shoot you to rag tatters."

Wild Bill watched Brennan turn it over and over rapidly, looking at all the angles. Wild Bill knew he would crater. Brennan's type could show genius at scheming, but were cowards in their heart of hearts. Bill was also confident that Brennan was *not* the judge of men, nor the handler of them, that he thought he was. That's why Bill was taking this second calculated risk.

"It's a deal," Brennan agreed. "But I still think you'd be smarter to take a cut."

"I'm satisfied this way," Hickok assured him. He stood up, and Brennan saw the rope coiled in his left hand.

"Get back in bed, Gina," Wild Bill ordered the blonde. "You two are going to be tied up together while I vacate the premises. I'll loop you front to front—won't that be pleasant?"

When he had them tied up, and gagged with strips of sheet, Bill placed the muzzle of his sixshooter against Brennan's left temple.

"You call off your dogs *today*, is that clear? Or I swear on the Hickok family bones I'll ride back and put you down like a sick animal. Do you believe me?"

Clearly Brennan still couldn't understand how Hickok could be so peacock vain. They were strange terms, and a damned nuisance. But while a temporary setback, calling off this one job wasn't the end of either Gil's freedom or his operation.

He nodded his head, and a moment later Hickok was gone.

* * *

Toward suppertime that night Wild Bill Hickok finally returned to Beecher's Station, saddle-ragged and sleepy, leading the sorrel and riding a ginger mare he'd stolen from Brennan.

Josh gave him the hail from up on the roof. "All quiet here, Bill. You find Brennan?"

Bill nodded, swinging down and turning his horses over to Yancy.

"I talked to him," Hickok affirmed, pausing to light a cheroot that had gone out.

"Just talked?" Yancy probed, sounding disappointed.

"If I played it right," Bill assured him, "Brennan is either already dead or will be soon. How's Jimmy making?"

"Says he's feeling sparky," Josh reported. "Called you a yellow-bellied sapsucker and said he prayed God you'd die hard at Brennan's."

Bill laughed and shook his head. "He's back to normal, God help us."

"There's hot corn bread and soup ready inside," Josh added. "Man alive, that Charlene ain't just pretty as four aces, Bill. She can cook. And nurse? Why, she's got thank-you letters from Clara Barton for her work during the war! She's some pumpkins, all right."

Bill was heading into the burned-out shell at the front of the station, his Winchester over one shoulder. "Invite me to the wedding, kid."

"I didn't mean anything like that," Josh flung back down.

Yancy followed Wild Bill inside. "I got the wheel trued, Bill, and I put some temporary bracings on the worst-damaged parts of the coach. I also gave the harness rig a close inspection. It's in good shape."

" 'Preciate it." Bill spotted Charlene working over a big cookstove in the kitchen. She wore a pretty yellow dress with her hair again drawn into its neat coil. She spotted him, smiled that restive, mysterious smile of hers, and looked away again.

Bill headed on toward Jimmy's room. "Yancy, where's Burl?"

"We're keeping two men on guard now. He's out by the corral."

Wild Bill nodded. "Good thinking. Tonight we're gonna keep that up—two men on guard, two men sleeping. We'll be pulling out at sunup. Take Joshua's place, will you, and send him inside to Jimmy's room."

"Christ, heal my eyes," Jimmy complained the moment Wild Bill stepped into his room. "I had you dead by now."

"You look good, old roadster. Ready to fight?"

"Got my color back," Jimmy quipped, and they both laughed. Joshua entered, Jimmy's rifle under his arm.

"So is Brennan dead?" Jimmy asked.

Bill shook his head. "Like I just told the kid, he was alive when I left him. But I don't think he will be for long."

Hickok explained his arrangement with Gil Brennan. Jimmy started smiling even before Bill had finished. Joshua, however, as Brennan himself had, seemed puzzled.

"But how's that settle anything?" he demanded. "Even if he does call his men off this time?"

Jimmy, propped up by pillows, answered for Hickok. "Oh, he'll sure-God *try* to call his men off. But Sandy Urbanski and Rick Collins won't pull back now. It was Leland reminded us of something—both of them once rode with Quantrill and his butchering mob."

Bill nodded. "Brennan is a fool, thinks he can ride herd on them. But I predict Urbanski will kill him and take over this job himself."

"What then?" Josh asked.

"That has to play out, kid. But the point is that the brains of the operation will be dead. If we three can handle the brawn, Overland's problem will be solved. And even if I'm wrong, and Brennan ain't killed today—I meant what I told him about the law catching up to him now that prosecutors are setting up shop out here."

Jimmy tested his leg. "It'll take my weight. We pulling out tomorrow?"

Bill nodded. "You've already cost us a day, you sorry sack of dung. But tonight could get lively, too, depending what happens and how they decide to play it. We might have a full-bore attack right here, and we'll have to be ready for it. Right now, though, I'm wrapping my teeth around some grub."

Before Bill and Josh could leave, however, Jimmy said, "J. B.?"

Hickok was instantly alerted. Jimmy seldom called him by his real initials except for serious subjects.

"Yeah?"

142

"While you was gone and I was under? I—ahh, had the queerest dream, if that's what you'd call it. You was playing poker in Deadwood. Place called the Number 10 Saloon. I ain't never been to Deadwood. Is there a watering hole by that name?"

Wild Bill nodded, his face completely blank. "There is. So many saloons in Deadwood, they just decided to number them."

"Maybe I heard that before," Jimmy said, mostly to himself, "and maybe I just forgot it."

"Maybe." Wild Bill could feel Joshua staring at him, but he ignored the kid. "So that's it? I was playing poker in the Number 10? Was I winning?"

"I . . . yeah, seems there was yaller boys piled up front of you. I do remember that you was holding aces and eights."

Bill, still steady and calm, nonetheless paled slightly. And Joshua felt his blood seem to change course in his veins. Aces and eights . . . the hand Calamity Jane swore Bill would be holding when he was murdered—in Deadwood.

"It's the damndest thing, too," Jimmy added, "but the ace of spaces was *red*. Just like . . ."

Jimmy trailed off at the look on Joshua's face. "Damn foolish dreams," he added. "Don't mean nothing."

143

Chapter Fourteen

"You boys just wait right out here in the yard," Sandy Urbanski told Collins and the rest. "I'll go inside and see what he wants. Keep your eyes open. Brennan had two of his ranch hands killed last night, both throat-slashed Apache fashion. Had to be Hickok. He might still be around."

Sandy swung down from the saddle and tossed his reins to Dobber Ulrick to hold for him. His boot heels thumped loudly on the raw planks of the front porch. Brennan's Chinese house boy opened the front door and led Urbanski back through a luxuriously appointed living room to an even more splendid library.

"Sandy," Brennan greeted him, rising from a leather easy chair where he had been sitting, drinking rye whiskey and staring into the snapping flames of a fieldstone fireplace.

"So this is how the upper crust lives," Sandy said, gazing around at the leather-bound books and heavy teak furniture. He also aimed a contemptuous glance at Brennan's velvet smoking jacket.

"Take a load off, Sandy," Brennan invited, motioning toward a chair near the fire. "Whiskey?"

"I could cut the phlegm."

Brennan poured a few fingers of rye into a pony glass and handed it to his hireling. "Good Cuban cigars in that humidor beside you," he added.

Urbanski helped himself to several, putting one in his mouth and a few more in his shirt pocket. "This ain't the reception I was expecting, boss," he admitted. "Figured you called me in here to read me the riot act."

"What, you mean because you haven't finished the job yet?"

Urbanski nodded, watching his boss through curls of strong, fragrant smoke.

"Don't know how's I blame you for that," Brennan assured him. "Hickok's been one step ahead of *both* of us all the way. My plan to plant him at Martin's Creek failed. Your ambush failed. My plan to blow the slope, the fake heist diversion—he's had a fox play for every move we try."

"You're sure mighty philosophical about it all of a sudden. I thought you was hot to heist this gold."

Brennan knocked back another jolt of liquor.

He seemed edgy, expectant, and Urbanski started watching him close.

"Look," he pressed his boss, "is this heist still on, r'not?

"Sandy, I'm not God in the universe. If Hickok has outsmarted us, is it wise to keep pushing a thing that won't move?"

"You're not God in . . . You know what, Brennan? You're so full of shit, your feet are sliding. You better spell it out plain for me. The hell you trying to say here?"

Brennan, too nervous to sit still, got up and stood looking into the fire. Hickok's surprise visit this morning had been playing in his mind all day. At first he had only agreed to call off this job out of fear of Hickok. But the things Wild Bill said had been gnawing at him all day.

Don't you know there's prosecutors already out west, taking depositions and putting fellows like you in prison—or worse?

"Sandy," he began in a reasonable tone, "there's an old saying: The bucket went once too often to the well. You know, we only decided on this gold-robbing scheme because there's damn little law in place out here right now. But that doesn't mean we can operate at will. There's rumors about federal prosecutors coming out here, taking depositions and—"

"Why, you mealymouthed coward," Urbanski cut in. "Hickok *was* here, wasn't he? He's put snow in your boots and now you're turning squaw on us?"

"Don't talk to me like that in my own home," Brennan warned, his voice going tight.

Something reckless and scared in that voice warned Urbanski. He stood up, turned Brennan around by one shoulder, and threw a quick uppercut at the point of his jaw. The blow staggered Brennan but didn't knock him out. Clutching his boss by the front of his jacket, Urbanski searched his eyes.

"Well, cuss my coup," he finally said. "You're trying to screw up the courage to kill me, you white-livered little weak sister."

He plunged his hand into Brennan's breast pocket and found the two-shot derringer.

"You damn little poodle," Urbanski snarled. "Thought you could whip a full-growed dog with *this* peashooter. Here, I'll show you—"

Brennan gathered his strength to tear away, but Urbanski suddenly shot him with both barrels, low in the belly so the dying would be painful.

Because of the thick stone walls, the gunshots were not loud enough to disturb the men out in the bunkhouse. But the houseboy fled in terror, and those milling in the front yard came rushing inside. They found Urbanski in the library, smoking a cigar and grinning in triumph. Brennan lay sprawled in a pool of his own blood, making incoherent whimpering sounds.

Sandy looked round at each man: Rick Collins, Dobber Ulrick, AJ Clayburn and Waco McKinney.

"I'm taking the reins from here, boys," he announced. "Same terms as before: equal shares on the gold. And we quit pussyfootin' around.

We hit 'em as they pull out in the morning. You ready to ride?"

One by one they all nodded. Urbanski jerked a thumb toward the liquor cabinet. "Good. Help yourselves."

Collins nodded toward the dying man. "What about him? You just leaving the body here?"

"We'll take it with us, dump him someplace where the carrion birds will take care of him. Let's hump it, boys. We got forty miles to cover before morning. I know a good spot where we can hit 'em right as they leave Beecher's Station."

"There's one thing you ain't saying, Urbanski," Waco spoke up quick. "Ain't you gonna tell us how Hickok is all *yours*, don't nobody else kill him?"

"That's it," Dobber agreed. "It's all you was saying 'fore we started this job."

Sudden anger, barely controllable, made Urbanski's face flush with blood. But he quickly remembered that Brennan's fate could easily be turned on him, too. Dobber's right hand hung beside his knee, ready to seize the throwing knife in his boot.

"All right, I'll say it," he told them all with no flinching. "Hickok's more man than I gave him credit for. But are *you* fools telling me he made dead men drive that coach yesterday?"

All of them looked foolish and lowered their gazes.

"All right, then," Sandy gloated. "He sent alla you running like a pack of scalded dogs. Now's your chance to see if you got a set on you. I got three exploding arrows reserved for him, and I still mean to be the one who kills him."

Sandy paused for a moment, distracted by the loud clogged-drain noise as Brennan gave up the ghost.

"But we've wasted enough time, boys, and it's time to get this job over. Brennan was right on one thing. It's lawing-up all over nowadays. Circuit judges, penny-a-mile arrest fees. Let's get this gold and head south for a while—I know a good place near Vera Cruz. First, though, we settle Hickok's hash, and I don't care *who* gets it done. I don't mind going shares on the reward, either. We can stop on our way to Old Mex, trade his head for that ten thousand dollars."

Burl and Yancy drew the last stint of guard duty. About one hour before sunrise, Burl's nervous, high-pitched voice raised the alarm from on top of the station:

"Riders comin'! Heading in from northeast of here!"

Charlene Durant, pleasantly exhausted, gave a little yawp of alarm when Wild Bill sat up in bed, almost causing her to slide naked onto the floor.

"Sorry," Bill told her as he stepped quickly into his trousers, then buckled on his gunbelt. "Kid, you up?" he called out.

"Both of us are!" Jimmy's voice replied from out front. "You're the one ain't at his post, Romeo!"

"Obviously everyone knows where you slept last night," Charlene lamented.

Bill snorted. "I didn't 'sleep' any more than you did."

"That a complaint?"

Bill kissed her. "That was a brag. You better get dressed."

Wild Bill joined the others in the dark chill of the yard. "How many, Burl?" he called up. "And how far?"

"I counted at least five, Bill, with a string of remounts. Could be more—they're kicking up plenty of dust. Still a couple miles out, just crossing Timber Ridge."

"If they've got remounts, then they've been to Brennan's ranch," Bill surmised. "They riding straight on us?"

"Un-uh. Bearing west."

Jimmy, sitting on the water casket to favor his wounded leg, looked at Bill in the gathering light. "Sunrise attack?"

Hickok nodded. "I was looking for it, so I scouted the terrain yesterday before I rode to Brennan's place. Just northwest of here is a series of natural-erosion cutbanks. That's where they're headed to take up positions. Josh?"

"Yeah?"

"Run out to the coach and dig out my field glasses, wouldja? And then saddle up the sorrel for me."

Bill got a kerosene lantern from inside and set it on the water casket beside Jimmy. In the light he checked his loads.

"You gonna need my eyes for this?" Jimmy asked.

Wild Bill shook his head as he stuffed one pocket with extra centerfire cartridges for his rifle. "You just go easy on that leg. I got it figured. Whether or not they've killed Brennan, the whole bunch of them are getting nervous. I planted one idea—prosecution in the courts. Now they're fed up with the cat-and-mouse game, they want to put paid to it. But I'm going to spoil this attack before they can make it. Force them to hit us on open road. The more desperate they are to get it over with, the more they'll lose their battle discipline."

The sorrel was ready. Wild Bill tied his Winchester with the cantle straps, then swung up and over, reining the animal around to the north.

"The rest of you," he called out, "take the best cover you can in case this is another trick. I don't think they'll attack the station again—they know we're ready. Burl?"

"Yeah?"

"You all right?"

"Sure, I'm sober, Bill."

"How 'bout Charlene? There an extra weapon for her?"

"I've got it already," she informed them, stepping out into the yard. The old Henry rifle she carried was almost as long as she was.

"I loaded it for her and showed her how to use it," Burl explained.

"She might not hit anything," Bill joked, "but

since it's a Henry at least she won't need reloading for a week."

By the time Hickok reached a long, low rise overlooking the cutbanks, a salmon-pink edge of sunlight showed in the east. Bill swung down, left the sorrel hobbled below the crest of the ridge, and carried his rifle and field glasses up to the crest, low-crawling the last thirty yards to cut his skyline.

He had called it right except for the timing. He had to work quickly if he wanted to strike before the lead rider was safe within the cutbanks.

Hickok levered a round into the chamber, then reached back and pulled off one of his boots. Lying as flat as he could, he used the boot to prop his muzzle just up off the ground.

Now came the tricky part, but Wild Bill had done it once before when temporary snow blindness ruined his vision one winter in Niobrara County, Nebraska. Colonel Cody had once told Bill that extraordinary shooters could *feel* a bullet's trajectory without the assistance of normal aiming.

Bill focused the field glasses until he had the lead rider sharply imaged. It was Sandy Urbanski—he recognized him from Leland's description of the knife scar.

"Damnitall anyway," Hickok cursed when Urbanski made it to safety before he could shoot. But the second rider, a skinny, mean-looking cur wearing scarred-up cowboy chaps, was not so lucky. Bill's first shot turned the rider in his saddle; the second knocked him off his horse.

Quickly, before the men behind him could scatter to the rear, Wild Bill focused in on another rider, a lanky man wearing the shapeless flop hat of a hillman. His first bullet wiped the man out of the saddle.

Two men down, and Hickok had accomplished his mission. The frightened men would not be able to stage for an attack right away. True, Urbanski had made it to the cutbanks, but he wouldn't have the guts to attack on his own. More time lost as he regrouped his men and came up with another plan.

Wild Bill scuttled back down to his horse, thumbed reloads into his rifle, then tied it behind the saddle again. He slipped off the hobbles, then swung up and over, reining the sorrel back around toward what was left of Beecher's Station.

It was a nice bit of sniping, Bill congratulated himself. And if no more men joined them, he had also cut the odds down in their favor. Either they'd call it off now, or there'd be one more attack—out on the open flats where retreat would not be an option.

Chapter Fifteen

"All set!" Yancy hollered from under the coach, crawling out with the grease pail in his hand. "The horses are tied secure and the axles and hubs greased."

Wild Bill, atop the box with the reins in his gloved hands, nodded at the burly blacksmith. " 'Preciate it, Yancy. It's going to take Overland time to clear the stage road at Devil's Slope. You boys hang on here. It's high time this boil was lanced, and it soon will be."

Jimmy, his wounded leg stretched out straight, occupied the box beside Wild Bill. Hickok had ordered Joshua to ride inside the coach with Charlene—an order he didn't have to repeat. Lovesick little pup, Bill thought, although he also had to admit that he couldn't blame the kid. As women went, Charlene Du-

154

rant rated aces high. But again he felt the niggling certainty he knew her from somewhere.

Bill was about to crack the popper of his blacksnake when Burl, standing guard on the roof, called out:

"Rider coming from the east, Wild Bill! I think I recognize that buckskin he's riding. . . . Hell yes, it's Lanny Johnson, an express rider from the Overland office in Rapid City. Best hold up a minute."

The rider, his horse lathered from the pace, hailed Wild Bill with the usual, "Touch you for luck?" and handshake. He reached up from the saddle, just below Bill's level, and handed him a folded yellow telegram.

"It's from Allan Pinkerton in Denver," Lanny explained. "Mr. Langford said to tell you he's been in regular touch with him. Giving him details to check out."

"So Leland knows about the rockslide?"

"I'll say he knows! Stages are backing up there until a work gang clears it."

Wild Bill nodded his thanks, then unfolded the brief message and read it. His brow was suddenly troubled although that passed quickly as he became more thoughtful. He folded the message and stuck it in the pocket of his canvas duster. "Thanks, Lanny."

"Bad news?" Jimmy said beside him.

"Can't see any way to call it good," Bill replied. "And it might be damn bad."

Jimmy shook his head. "You ever give a straight answer in your life, Bill?"

"No," Bill declared straight, and both men laughed.

"What's the telegram say?" Josh demanded, hanging out one of the windows.

"It says mind your own damn beeswax, junior," Wild Bill called back. And before the kid could pester him some more, Hickok cracked his whip and shouted the team into motion.

"I figure Urbanski has had time to rabbit by now," Bill advised Jimmy. "But watch careful when we draw near those cutbanks."

"What, you think I'll sleep if you don't nag me, mother?" Jimmy shot back. "Lord, how could a fool this big be so famous?"

"Besides," Bill added with a sly grin, "according to your dream, I'll cop it in Deadwood over a poker table."

"Bad luck to talk about it," Jimmy dismissed him, losing his grin, which made Hickok laugh louder.

"Cow plop," he teased his friend. "So what if your dream's true, hanh? When you meet the man who's going to live forever, please send me his name."

"I'll send you a cat's tail if you don't shut up."

They kept up their verbal sparring even as they passed the cutbanks without incident. For perhaps twenty miles the coach covered mostly level terrain, once-lush grass now browning with the autumn frosts. Twice they spotted herd cattle in the distance, some Longhorn stock but most of them the newer Shorthorn and white-faced Hereford breeds.

"Dust puffs up ahead," Jimmy remarked

some time around midmorning. "Way up ahead—seen 'em yet?"

Bill shook his head and took his field glasses off the board seat beside him. "Now I do. Hard to say how many men since they've got remounts sending up dust, too."

"Might not even be them," Jimmy suggested, though he didn't sound convinced.

Thus distracted, both men had paid scant attention to an old abandoned manure wagon that sat rotting about two hundred yards off the trail to their right, in an old cornfield now stubbled with short, dry stalks. Bill had seen it and given it a cursory inspection. But with no horse in sight, nor any place to hide one, he didn't rate the wagon as a serious threat. That was one of his few mistakes on this entire mission, he realized later in useless hindsight.

Not until Jimmy suddenly remarked, "Check out them cows at three o'clock, Bill. One of 'em's a blood bay horse," did Hickok abruptly reclassify the wagon as a threat. But even as he did, Sandy Urbanski rose on one knee, and Bill heard the powerful *fwip* of the crossbow releasing.

The explosive arrow drilled into the box on Jimmy's side, and then glowing chunks of wood peppered Wild Bill and Jimmy like canister shot.

"Jerusalem!" Jimmy exclaimed, struggling to pivot so he could get off a shot. But his wounded leg was virtually useless for bending. Not only that, but his shirt was on fire in two places.

Judd Cole

Bill swiped at Jimmy, pushing him down so he was a smaller target and to smother the flames. Dropping the reins, he pivoted half right on the board seat and opened fire on the wagon with his Winchester. The weapon kicked into his shoulder repeatedly, brass casings glinting in the sunlight as they sprayed out the ejector port.

"Chuck up the team!" he called to Jimmy. "Urbanski took a chance leaving his horse so far away. But he knows damn well we can't get at him across that open ground."

Jimmy spirited the team on while Wild Bill kept up his fire, forcing Urbanski to cover down close. But as the range lengthened and the angle went against Bill, Urbanski got in one last lick: Hickok heard a sickening thump, then a hideous death shriek from the sorrel horse tied at the back of the coach. Urbanski had managed to sink an exploding arrow deep in the horse's right flank, killing it almost instantly.

The dragging weight slowed the coach, and Jimmy quickly reined in, heaving into the brake. With Jimmy covering, Joshua leaped quickly outside and freed the dead animal from the coach.

Not long after they started rolling southwest again, Joshua called up topside: "I see their game, Bill! Urbanski's following us way back. The other two are up ahead. Classic pincers."

"Pincers," Wild Bill agreed. "They're going to try a rolling squeeze. They haven't got enough manpower to just rush us in the open. But they're going to count on their speed and ma-

neuverability. Plink away at us, then close in
like wolves on a buff."

"I'm going to work on Urbanski," Jimmy
vowed, hauling himself up onto the roof behind
the box and flattening down. "If I can't hit the
son of a bitch, least I can keep him shy."

"Joshua!" Bill called down. "I need you to
poke your head out the left-side window now
and then, give me a report what's up ahead.
Jimmy's occupied to our back trail. But don't
leave your head hanging out in the wind, boy.
Just poke it out, look, get it back inside. Charlene?"

"Yes, Bill?"

"Come forward off the seat, and get as low on
the floor as you can. There's going to be shooting behind—"

But even before Wild Bill could finish, a
round punched through the back of the coach.
Charlene shrieked, then quickly reported it was
all right, just close.

"Too damn close," Jimmy agreed, squeezing
off a shot at Urbanski. "Maybe I can drop his
horse."

But Urbanski had plenty of experience running down conveyances, and he knew just how
far he needed to drop back to thwart a good
shooter on a wildly rocking coach. He had put
his crossbow aside now in favor of a rifle, and
the three-hundred-grain bullets found the
coach with discouraging regularity.

As quickly as his rifle emptied, Jimmy re-
loaded from his bandolier. But he was forced to
halt, after his third reload, when the rifle over-

heated, due to rate of fire, and a casing hung up during ejection. Jimmy cleared it while Wild Bill heard another bullet go whiffing past his right ear.

As if on a blood scent, Urbanski sensed trouble and sank steel into his gelding, spurting closer for a better shot. Wild Bill heard the hoofs drumming faster behind them and called to Jimmy: "Heads up! He's closing!"

Wild Bill side-armed his rifle up to Jimmy's position, and the sharpshooter, despite using a sight adjusted for Bill's aim, was able to drop Urbanski's horse with his second bullet. At that speed, the rider catapulted over the animal's head, hit the trail hard, then bounced along like a sack of rags until his momentum wore out.

"Hell, he's still alive," Jimmy complained, but before he could drop a bead on Urbanski, the savvy survivor scurried back behind his dead horse.

"It's all right, you done good, Jimmy," Wild Bill praised him. "Hell, I'm starting to enjoy this."

Eventually realizing that Urbanski had gone down, the two men out front split wide on the flanks, circling around to take him a remount and thus losing more time.

"To hell with that," Bill decided suddenly, tossing the reins to Jimmy again. "Haze those flankers off for me, James," Bill added as he started down off the box. Jimmy had freed the stoppage in his rifle by now, so Bill grabbed his Winchester back.

With pursuit broken, Bill had reined in the team to blow, so it was quick work to slip behind the coach and untie the lineback dun he had selected back at Martin's Creek Station. This horse was the natural "cow pony" of the American West, prized for its ability to dodge and cut.

Jimmy couldn't keep those flank men off forever, so Bill hurried, not bothering with saddle or rigging, just leaping on bareback and clutching fistfuls of mane. He held his Winchester under one arm, lowering himself over the horse's neck to reduce target.

Bill wore no spurs, but urged the lineback to a powerful gallop, breaking the line of approach by hurling his weight to right and left, sending the mount sharply swerving.

Urbanski, still hunkered behind his dead horse, kept up an unrelenting fire at Wild Bill. The lineback flinched when a slug grazed its flank, but then drove powerfully forward, lowering its weight and lengthening its stride. Now Wild Bill slid down the left side of the horse, hanging on with one arm and one leg, using just his left hand to bring his rifle up.

Bill was hurtling at his enemy, barely able to sustain a line of fire. Urbanski, his hard-bitten eyes now engulfed with panic, came up in a crouch and loosed several shots at Wild Bill's horse.

Perhaps twenty yards out from Urbanski's position, Wild Bill heard the sickening thud of a bullet impacting, felt the lineback shudder in midstride. To avoid being trapped under the

161

falling horse, Wild Bill let go and pushed off with one muscular leg.

Even before he hit the ground hard, Wild Bill's brain was calculating. He let his rifle go, and because he had already loosened the riding thongs, he remembered to clap his hands to his Colts and keep them in the holsters while he tumbled and skidded to a stop.

Skin rubbed off hard as he scraped along, but Wild Bill never even came to a full stop before he shot up to his feet, drawing his pistols.

But he never had to fire one bullet. Fear now had Urbanski by the wits. He stood up, turned, and began running desperately to stay out of short-gun range.

Urbanski's right foot suddenly plunged into a prairie-dog hole, and he went down to the ground hard, his Winchester Yellow Boy flying from his hands and crashing down too. And thanks to that worn sear Urbanski had kept neglecting, it discharged almost point-blank in his face.

Hickok flinched when he heard the hideous screaming, saw Urbanski writhing furiously like a snake trapped under a wheel, clutching his ravaged face. When he flopped over on his back, Wild Bill winced at the damage: That high-power slug had blown half Urbanski's lower jaw off, including most of his lower teeth.

Bill took pity and finished him quick with a slug behind the ear.

That shot also broke the back of the gold heist plot. Both men on the flanks, seeing Urbanski die like a dog in the road, split up and retreated back to the north country and the shelter of the Black Hills. They were finished—Bill knew now that Brennan must be dead. And with Urbanski soon to be colder than a wagon wheel himself, there was no one left to ramrod another gang.

Seeing Bill's downed horse, Jimmy turned the team and went back to pick up their driver. Josh leaped out and ran on ahead.

"Bill!" he called out. "You all right?"

As Josh came up beside him, breathless from running, Wild Bill pointed over his shoulder without looking back. "I'm a sight better off than Urbanski," he replied.

"Man alive!" Josh nattered on, so excited he could barely keep his words in order. "You were unbelievable, Bill! It was a classic charge, you—"

Wild Bill cut the kid off by raising one hand. The coach had almost reached them. Charlene's pretty face hung out the window, worried sick.

"Tell me straight," Bill said quickly. "You're in love with her, are'n'cha?"

Josh started, taken completely aback, then answered Bill's question by flushing crimson. Over the past year, Josh had developed "cases" for several of the beauties in Bill's ample stable. But even Hickok recognized that Charlene was different.

"I'm not faulting your taste, Longfellow," Wild Bill said as he drew the telegram from his pocket and handed it over to Joshua. "But before you start thinking matrimony, might be a good idea to read this. It's from Pinkerton."

The excitement of their running battle now

bled from Joshua's face as he read the disturbing news:

JAMIE: GENERAL DURANT CONFIRMS DAUGHTER NAMED CHARLENE. BUT SHE'S HAPPILY MARRIED TO A CLERGYMAN IN MONROE, MICHIGAN, NOW MRS. CHARLENE BRANDENBERG. CAUTION ADVISED.

Josh stared at Wild Bill, his face blank. "Then . . . who is this woman?"

"More to the point, kid, *what* is she?"

"Brennan," Joshua said, not making it a question.

"My first thought, too," Wild Bill said. "But if she was hired by him, why didn't she make her play and kill me? She had the chance. Now it's too late."

"What are you two telling secrets about?" Charlene demanded as Jimmy pulled the stagecoach up.

"Mainly," Bill told her amiably, "we were trying to guess your real name. I make you for a Sally or maybe an Abigail?"

The woman who called herself Charlene Durant flushed deeply, staring at the telegram in Joshua's hand.

"Who told you?" she said in a weak voice.

"Sally?" Bill pressed. "Abigail? Darlene?"

"It's Clarissa," she confessed. "Clarissa Charbonnet."

"Well, God kiss me," Wild Bill muttered, at the same time that Joshua met his eyes and exclaimed, "Man alive! It *is* her! The long hair fooled me."

"That's where I saw you before," Wild Bill told her. "It was in St. Louis, back in '71. A play called *The Merry Widow*."

"My last public appearance," she admitted. "Obviously both of you already know why."

As did half the people in America. *The Merry Widow*, a wildly popular comedy about a gold-digging widow, had made Clarissa a household name. But when she fell in love with the leading male actor, who was married, the resulting affair and scandal got her banned from the stage. She became the favorite "painted Jezebel" of the press, hounded everywhere she went by "decency committees."

"So you headed west to start over," Wild Bill said. "What in the hell made you pose as Durant's daughter? How'd you even know about her?"

"We went to boarding school together near Chicago, then later she became one of my biggest admirers, and we corresponded regularly. I was frightened to travel by myself. I hoped that claiming the general was my father might . . . dissuade disreputable men from . . ."

She trailed off, but her point was clear enough.

Joshua was grinning, relief evident in his face. Jimmy, completely in the dark, stared down at all of them. "We going to hold a camp meeting here?" he demanded. "Or get this damned gold to Denver?"

Epilogue

"Exter! Exter! Read all about it!" shouted a corner newsboy as Wild Bill and Joshua walked the final block of Union Street leading to the Denver train depot. "Read all about it right heah, folks! Wild Bill Hickok defeats last Black Hills crime gang! Ter-r-*riffic* sensation, read it he-ah!"

Joshua carried a big leather valise. Wild Bill led his beloved strawberry roan, Fire-away, by the bridle. The gelding had been stalled for weeks and kept nudging Bill impatiently, eager to get running. Everything Hickok owned was now packed into two big saddle panniers.

"Had to happen sooner or later, kid," Wild Bill consoled him. "Hell, you're the top newspaper writer in the country. You think they were gonna leave you out here to die among the tumbleweeds? You came out here a greenantlered dude who couldn't tell gee from haw. Now you're not only savvy—you're a young Charlie Dickens."

The praise made Josh's cheeks glow with pride, but he still hadn't accepted the news yet: Without so much as a kiss-me-Kate, the *New York Herald* had called him back. And despite the fact that he was being "promoted to the masthead" of the editorial staff, he felt he was being punished for doing excellent work.

Jimmy, however, had left much more cheerfully yesterday, collecting his pay and taking the first eastbound train. He was returning to Tupelo, Mississippi, to visit his family, who were sharecropping there for their former master. Though he said nothing about it, both men knew Jimmy was planning on turning over the bulk of his pay to them. That fact, Bill told Josh, impressed him even more than Jimmy's shooting.

"See how it works, Bill?" Joshua fumed. "*See* how talent gets you in trouble?"

Hickok laughed and had to take the cigar from his mouth. "Uhh—yeah, I've known about that for some time, kid."

Joshua flushed as he felt the point. "What I mean is—they'll stick me in a ten-story building, and I'll spend the rest of my life wearing green eyeshades and moving commas around."

"Sure, by day. But by candlelight you'll write great books," Bill assured him. "Books that will make the American West practically talk to the reader, it'll seem so alive. You were *here*, kid, and there's western dirt under your nails that'll never wash out. Don't ever forget, you learned it all straight from the best. I took a blank slate and filled it proper."

"Yeah! I did learn from the best, didn't I?" Josh said, more to himself than Wild Bill. "How to ride and shoot and fight with my fists. How to find water where it ain't and read sign like an Apache—"

"*Almost* like an Apache," Bill corrected him, and they both laughed.

"You know," Josh hinted, just probing for his friend's reaction, "no law forces me to go back. I can quit the Herald, stay out west as a freelance stringer. That way I could keep telling your story."

"My story," Bill said in his usual amiable way as they came abreast of the depot, "is about to play out, Josh."

But his tone couldn't cancel out his meaning, and as Bill's gunmetal gaze held the kid's for a long moment, Josh felt his scalp tingle with a premonition of something he didn't want to know.

"Now I get it," he blurted out. "That's why you wouldn't say where you're going. You're headed to Deadwood, right?"

"Might head up that way, sure."

"But why?" Josh demanded. "I mean . . . Calamity Jane's prediction, Jimmy's dream . . ."

"So what about 'em? Since when does J. B. Hickok turn giddy when the talk goes to death and dying? Can you remember a time?"

Josh had to shake his head. "Only thing I ever

saw that truly scared you to run away was Calamity Jane."

"That much I admit, boy. She scares me foolish."

The eyes watching Joshua did not look sad or frightened or regretful. Bill's face was calm, at peace, the look of a man who had quit fighting his destiny—let it come, he embraced it without apology or regret.

"Josh," he said, "I'll tell you straight-arrow why I'm heading to Deadwood alone. You've been with me through hell and high water. Never once did you ever let me down when it mattered. Son, I've ridden with the best men in America, and I'm here to tell you: I *never* rode with a better man than Joshua Robinson of Philadelphia. You're a credit to your dam."

A huge, hard lump of pride and feeling pinched Joshua's throat shut.

"But way I see it now," Hickok resumed, "I just don't want you around to see the rest of it— the part that don't matter. Do you take my drift, kid? I don't want that nothing part to be in your memory. You're going to live a long, happy life, kid. You're going to get married, bounce little brats on your knee. I want only the good times, the exciting times when your blood was thrumming and you never felt so alive—that's what I want you to take from the time when your trail crossed Bill Hickok's. You clear on that?"

Josh only nodded, not trusting his voice. Bill was calm and deliberate, and Josh copied him, his hero.

"The dying ain't worth but a mention," Bill

169

finished up. "All I want you to remember is that Bill Hickok by-God *lived* more than any ten men, and he never regretted a day. You understand that, ink-slinger?"

Joshua, despite his determination, was damn close to spilling it like a blubbering schoolgirl. But he pulled himself up and grinned. "Understood."

Wild Bill winked as he swung up into leather. "Tell you something else. Some more useful advice. You'd *ought* to take a later train—maybe much later."

"Why?"

"Clarissa is registered at the Seton Arms Hotel under the name Sally Mason. She thinks mighty highly of you. I think you should stop by and see her."

"But you two—I mean—"

"Yeah, right, I was there, kid, I remember. But that's me and her. You and her is something else."

Josh said, "She did seem to really like me."

"On that pleasant note," Bill quipped, giving Fire-away a little nudge with his knees.

Josh stood there in the dusty, busy street, watching the greatest, bravest, toughest man he had ever known calmly ride off to meet his fate.

"Hey, Hickok!" Josh shouted.

Bill reined in and slewed around in the saddle. "Hey what?"

"You are *too* a perfumed dandy! I think Mrs. Hickok wanted a little girl!"

"Why, you damned mouthy pup! I'd whip the

snot outta you if I wasn't wearing my new shirt!"

Both men shared a final laugh. Then Wild Bill nodded once before touching a spur to his roan's flank, and Joshua watched him ride into the bloodred sunrise.

"Tell me how you die," he whispered, "and I'll tell you what you're worth."

WILD BILL

JUDD COLE

SANTA FE DEATH TRAP

All Wild Bill Hickok wants as he sets out for Santa Fe is a place to lie low for a while, to get away from the fame and notoriety that follows him wherever he goes. But fame isn't the only thing that sticks to Wild Bill like glue. He made a lot of enemies over the years. And one of them, Frank Tutt, has waited a good long time to taste sweet revenge. He knows Wild Bill is on his way to Santa Fe and he is ready for him . . . ready and eager to make him pay. But after all these years he can wait a bit longer, long enough to play a little game with his legendary target. Oh, he will kill Wild Bill, all right—but first he wants Bill to know what it is like to live in Hell.

___4720-9 $3.99 US/$4.99 CAN

WILD BILL

JUDD COLE

THE KINKAID COUNTY WAR

Wild Bill Hickok is a legend in his own lifetime. Wherever he goes his reputation with a gun precedes him—along with an open bounty of $10,000 for his arrest. But Wild Bill is working for the law when he goes to Kinkaid County, Wyoming. Hundreds of prime longhorn cattle have been poisoned, and Bill is sent by the Pinkerton Agency to get to the bottom of it. He doesn't expect to land smack dab in the middle of an all-out range war, but that's exactly what happens. With the powerful Cattleman's Association on one side and land-grant settlers on the other, Wild Bill knows that before this is over he'll be testing his gun skills to the limit if he hopes to get out alive.

___4529-X $3.99 US/$4.99 CAN

WILD BILL

YUMA BUSTOUT

JUDD COLE

When the Danford Gang terrorized Arizona, no one—not the U.S. Marshals or the Army—could bring them in. It took Wild Bill Hickok to do that. Only Wild Bill was able to put them in the Yuma Territorial Prison, where they belonged. But the prison can't hold them. The venomous gang escapes and takes the Governor's wife and her sister as hostages. So it is up to Wild Bill to track them down and do the impossible—capture the Danford Gang a second time. Only this time, the gang's ruthless leader, Fargo Danford, has a burning need for revenge against the one man who put him and the gang in prison in the first place, a need as deadly as the desert trap he has set for Bill.

___4674-1 $3.99 US/$4.99 CAN

WILD BILL

DEAD MAN'S HAND

JUDD COLE

Marshal, gunfighter, stage driver, and scout, Wild Bill Hickok has a legend as big and untamed as the West itself. No man is as good with a gun as Wild Bill, and few men use one as often. From Abilene to Deadwood, his name is known by all—and feared by many. That's why he is hired by Allan Pinkerton's new detective agency to protect an eccentric inventor on a train ride through the worst badlands of the West. With hired thugs out to kill him and angry Sioux out for his scalp, Bill knows he has his work cut out for him. But even if he survives that, he has a still worse danger to face—a jealous Calamity Jane.

___4487-0 $3.99 US/$4.99 CAN